THE OTHER SIDE
OF SILENCE

THE OTHER SIDE OF SILENCE

A NOVEL OF SUSPENSE

BILL PRONZINI

Walker & Company
New York

Published by Walker Publishing Company, Inc., New York

ISBN-13: 978-0-8027-1713-9

For Marcia

If we had a keen vision and feeling of all ordinary human life, it would be like hearing the grass grow and the squirrel's heart beat, and we should die of that roar which lies on the other side of silence.

—George Eliot

PART I
DEATH VALLEY

ONE

WHEN GEENA FINALLY LEFT him and filed for divorce, Fallon put the Encino house up for sale and took his last two weeks of vacation from Unidyne. Then he loaded the Jeep Liberty and drove straight to Death Valley.

Will Rodriguez was the only person he told where he was going. There was nobody else to tell, really. He had no close friends except for Will, and theirs was mostly a work-related friendship; and Timmy was three years gone now and his folks both dead, too. Geena could have guessed, of course. She knew him that well, though not nearly well enough to understand his reasons. She'd think the same thing she always did when he went to the desert. And she'd be wrong.

October was one of the Valley's best months. All months in the Monument were good, even July and August when the midday temperatures sometimes exceeded 120 degrees and Death Valley justified its Paiute Indian name, *Tomesha*—ground afire. If a sere desert climate held no terrors for you, if you respected it and accepted it on its terms, the attractions far outweighed the drawbacks.

Still, he'd always been partial to October, the early part of the month, so in that sense Geena's timing couldn't have been better. The beginning of the tourist season was still a month away, daytime temperatures seldom reached 100 degrees, and the constantly changing light show created by sun and wind and clouds was at its most spectacular. You could stay in one place all day, from dawn to dusk—Zabriskie Point, say, or the sand dunes near Stovepipe Wells—and with each ten-degree rise and fall of the sun, the colors of rock and sand hills changed from dark rose to burnished gold, from chocolate brown to purple and indigo and gray-black, with a spectrum of subtler shades in between.

It had been almost a year since he'd last been to the Valley. Much too long, but it had been a difficult year—the still-painful memories and the dying marriage and a heavy workload at Unidyne. He'd been alone on that last visit, as he was alone now; alone on the last dozen or so desert trips. Even before Timmy's death, Geena had refused to come with him anymore. She'd never much cared for desert country, actively disliked Death Valley, and she'd used Timmy as an excuse: he was too young, there were too many hazards, he was better off at home with her. After the accident, she hadn't needed an excuse anymore.

Well, he preferred being alone. Had always had loner tendencies, even during his stint in the army and the good early years with Geena before and after Timmy was born. The Valley was a place made for loners. You could share it only with someone who viewed it in the same perspective—not as endless miles of coarse, dead landscape but as a starkly beautiful wilderness teeming with life. To him it seemed almost sentient, as if deep within its ancient rock was something that approximated a soul.

He'd taken his time deciding where to go first on this trip. The Monument had more than three thousand square miles, second only among national parks to Yellowstone, and all sorts of terrain: the great trough of the Valley floor, with its miles of salt pan two hundred feet and more below sea level, its dunes and alluvial fans, its borate deposits and ancient borax works, its barren fields of gravel and broken rock, its five enclosing mountain ranges packed with hidden canyons, petroglyphs, played-out gold and silver mines, ghost towns.

Most of an evening had been spent with his topos, the topographical maps put out by the U.S. Geological Survey, before he finally settled on the Funeral Mountains and the Chloride Cliffs area. The Funerals formed one of the eastern boundaries, and their foothills and crests were laden not only with a variety of canyons but with the ruins of the Keane Wonder Mill and Mine and the gold boomtown of Chloride City.

He left the Jeep north of Scotty's Castle near Hells Gate, packed in, and stayed for three days and two nights. The first day was a little rough; even though regular gym workouts had kept him in good shape, it takes a while to refamiliarize yourself with desert mountain terrain after a year away. The second day was easier. He spent that one exploring Echo Canyon, then tramping among the thick-timbered tramways of the Keane and the decaying mill a mile below, where twenty stamps had processed eighteen hundred tons of ore a month in the 1890s. On the third day he climbed to the Funerals' sheer heights and Chloride City—no strain at all by then.

It was a good three days. He saw no other people except at a distance. Much of the tension and restless dissatisfaction slowly bled out of him. He could feel his spirits lifting again.

Geena was on his mind only once in those three days. Eleven years of marriage, all they'd shared and suffered through, and now she seemed almost a stranger. He didn't blame her for the long-running affair she'd finally admitted to, or leaving him to be with the other man; he hadn't been there for her, any more than she'd been there for him, in three long years. Maybe things would have been different if they'd had another child, but she wouldn't consider it, kept insisting she couldn't bear another loss after Timmy and the earlier miscarriage. There was a time when he'd thought so, but that was long past. The simple truth was, their life together had died when Timmy died. Now that they'd finally admitted it to each other, the only emotions he felt, and was sure she felt, were sadness and relief.

It was the morning of the third day, as he stood atop one of the crags looking out toward the Needle's Eye, when he thought of her. There was no wind and the stillness, the utter absence of sound, was so acute it created an almost painful pressure against the eardrums. Of all the things Geena hated about Death Valley, its silence—"void of silence," an early explorer had termed it—topped the list. It terrified her. On their last trip together, when she'd caught him listening, she'd said, "What are you listening *to*? There's nothing to hear in this godforsaken place. It's as if everything has shut down. Not just here—everywhere. As if all the engines have quit working."

Right. Exactly right. As if all the engines have quit working.

That, more than anything else, summed up the differences between them. To her, the good things in life, the essence of life itself, were people, cities, constant scurrying activity. She worshipped sensation and speed, needed to hear the steady, throbbing engines of civilization in order to feel safe, secure, alive.

He needed none of those things, needed *not* to hear the engines. Silence was what he craved. This kind of silence, nurturing, spiritual, that let him feel as he felt nowhere else, at ease with himself and his surroundings. It was the other kinds he hated, the cold, hurtful, destructive kind—the long, loud silences of a shattered marriage, the empty silence of a child's grave. They were worse than the thunder of engines.

He remembered something else Geena had said to him once, not so long ago. "When we were first together you were a fighter, Rick, a soldier in and out of uniform. You welcomed challenges, you faced problems and responsibilities head-on. But after Timmy died you just seemed to give up. Now all you want to do is run away and hide from the world."

Well, there was some truth in that. He'd been a fighter once, yes—the army had honed that tendency in him—but it had been more of necessity than choice. Like his drift into corporate security, the only well-paying job his four years of MP duty qualified him for, but work that didn't really satisfy him. He'd never felt comfortable in mainstream society. Cities and suburbs made him feel hemmed in, even though he'd lived in one or another most of his life. Too many complications, pressures, distractions. Traffic-clogged freeways, urban blight, random violence, gang-infested neighborhoods like the one he'd grown up in in East L.A. Those, and all the other by-products of what was laughingly called modern civilization: global warming, Nine-Eleven and the looming threat of terrorism, the stupid Iraq War.

Timmy's death had eroded the bonds that not only held him to Geena but to the hostile urban environment and a lifestyle that was mostly of her choosing and direction. Disenchanted, disaffected—he was both of those things. An escapist, too? Not the way Geena had meant it. He didn't want to hide from the world; he wanted to narrow it down to a better fit for Rick Fallon. And that meant open spaces, places without people, places without engines.

The desert country had a way of simplifying things, reducing life to an elemental and much more tolerable level. It cleansed your mind, allowed you to think clearly. Allowed you to breathe. It was in his blood; it kept calling him back. The one place he truly belonged.

This wasn't a new thought by any means. It was the main reason he'd taken the time off. Spend a couple of weeks in and around the Valley, reassure himself that the pull was strong enough to hold him permanently. And then quit Unidyne, quit Encino, start a whole new life. He wouldn't be able to live in the Monument—permanent residence was limited to a small band of Paiutes and Park Service employees—but he could find a place in one of the little towns in the Nevada desert, Beatty or Goldfield or Tonopah. Hire out as a guide, do odd jobs—whatever it took to support himself. Money wouldn't be a problem anyway; once the house and the rest of their joint possessions sold, he'd have several thousand dollars to fall back on.

Late that third afternoon he hiked back to where he'd left the Jeep. It had a sophisticated alarm system and he used the Club to lock the steering wheel, but they were habitual, city-bred precautions. He'd never had any trouble with thieves or vandals out here.

Before he crawled into his sleeping bag he sifted through the topos again to pick his next spot. He wasn't sure why he chose Manly Peak. Maybe because he hadn't been in the southern Panamints, through Warm Springs Canyon, in better than three years. Still, the region was not one of his favorites. A large portion of the area was under private claim, and the owners of the talc mines along the canyon took a dim view of trespassers. You had to be extra careful to keep to public lands when you packed in there.

Just before dawn he ate a couple of nutrition bars for breakfast, then pointed the Jeep down Highway 178. The sun was out by the time he reached the Warm Springs Canyon turnoff. The main road in was unpaved, rutted, and talc-covered—primarily the domain of eighteen-wheelers passing to and from the mines. You needed at least a four-wheel-drive vehicle to negotiate it and the even rougher trail that branched off of it. He wouldn't have taken a passenger car over one inch of that terrain. Neither would anyone else who knew the area or paid attention to the Park Service brochures, guidebooks, and posted signs.

That was why he was so surprised when he came on the Toyota Camry.

He'd turned off the main canyon road ten miles in, onto the trail into Butte Valley, and when he rounded a turn on the washboard surface there it was, pulled off into the shadow of a limestone shelf. No one visible inside or anywhere in the immediate vicinity.

He brought the Jeep up behind and went to have a look. All four of the

Toyota's tires were intact, a wonder given the road condition, but the car was no longer drivable. A stain that had spread out from underneath told him that the oil pan had been ruptured. The Camry had been there a while, at least two days; the look and feel of the oil stain proved that. He had to be the first person to come by since it was abandoned, or it wouldn't still be sitting here like this. Not many hikers or off-roaders ventured out this way in the off-season, the big ore trucks used the main canyon road, and there weren't enough park rangers for daily backcountry patrols.

The Toyota's side windows were so dust- and talc-caked that he could barely see through them. He tried the driver's door, found it unlocked. The interior was empty except for two things on the front seat. One was a woman's purse, open, the edge of a wallet poking out. The other was a piece of lined notepaper with writing on it in felt-tip pen, held down by the weight of the purse.

Fallon slid the paper free. On top was a date—Wednesday, two days ago—and the word "Dear" scratched out, as if the writer had decided there was no one to address the note to. Below that were several lines of shaky backhand printing. He sensed what it was even before he finished reading it.

> I can't go on anymore. There's no hope left. Court Spicer and his man Banning have seen to that. I'm sorry for everything and sick of all the hurt and trouble and it's too painful knowing I might never see Kevin again.

He couldn't quite decipher the scrawled signature. Casey or Cassy something. He opened the wallet and fanned through the card section until he found her driver's license. The Camry had California plates and the license had also been issued in the state. Casey Dunbar. Age 32. San Diego address. The face in the ID photo was attractive, light-haired, unsmiling.

The wallet contained half a dozen snapshots, all of a boy eight or nine years old. Fallon felt a wrenching sensation when he looked at them. The boy might have been Timmy if he'd lived to that age—different features but the same lean, smiling face, the same mop of fair hair falling over his forehead.

Nothing else in the wallet told him anything. One credit card was all Casey Dunbar owned. And twelve dollars in fives and singles.

Fallon returned the wallet to the purse, folded the note in there with it, and slid the purse out of sight under the seat. A set of keys dangled from the ignition; he removed them, locked the car before he pocketed them. In his mouth was a dryness that had nothing to do with the day's gathering heat.

If she'd brought along a gun or pills or some other lethal device, she was long dead by now. If she'd wanted the Valley to do the job for her, plenty enough time had elapsed for that, too, given the perilous terrain and the proliferation of sidewinders and daytime temperatures in the midnineties and no water and the wrong kind of clothing.

Yet there was a chance she was still alive. No carrion feeders in sight—a favorable sign, but not conclusive. It all depended on where she was.

All right. Alive or dead or dying, she had to be found, and quickly. He hurried back to the Jeep for his Zeiss binoculars.

TWO

HE CLIMBED UP ON the hood, made a slow scan of the surrounding terrain with the powerful 7×50 glasses. The valley floor here was flat- tish, mostly fields of fractured rock slashed by shallow washes. Clumps of low-growing creosote bush and turtleback were the only vegetation. He had an unobstructed look over a radius of several hundred yards.

No sign of her.

Some distance ahead there was higher ground. He drove too fast on the rough road, had to warn himself to slow down. At the top of a rise he stopped again and went to climb a jut of limestone to a notch in its crest. From there he had a much wider view, all the way to Striped Butte and the lower reaches of the Panamints.

The odds were against him spotting her, even with the binoculars. The topography's rumpled irregularity created too many hidden places; she might have wandered miles in any direction.

But he did locate her, and in less than ten minutes. Pure blind luck.

She was a quarter of a mile away to the southwest, in partial shade at the bottom of a salt-streaked wash. Lying on her side, motionless, knees drawn up fetally, face and part of her blonde head obscured by the crook of a bare arm. It was impossible to tell at this distance if she was alive or not.

The wash ran down out of the foothills like a long, twisted scar, close to the trail for a considerable distance, then hooking away from it in a gradual snake-track curve. Where she lay was at least four hundred yards from where he'd parked on the four-wheel track. He picked out a trail

landmark roughly opposite her position, then scrambled back down to
the Jeep.

His cell phone was in his pack. He dragged it out, switched it on. No signal. Sometimes you got one in the more remote sections of the Valley,
sometimes you didn't; out here, the ramparts of the Panamints must be
blocking it. No emergency help, then. Whether she was alive or dead, it was
up to him to deal with the situation.

It took him more than an hour to get to where she lay. Drive to the landmark, load his pack with two extra soft-plastic water bottles and the first-aid
kit, strap on the aluminum-framed pack, and then hike across humps and
flats of broken rock as loose and treacherous as talus. Even though the pre-
noon temperature was only in the eighties, he was sweating profusely—and
he'd used up a pint of water to replace the sweat loss—by the time he reached
the wash.

She still lay in the same drawn-up position. And she didn't stir at the
noises he made, the clatter of dislodged rocks, as he slid down the wash's
bank. He went to one knee beside her, groped for a sunburned wrist. Pulse,
faint and irregular. He didn't realize until then that he had been holding
his breath; he let it out thin and hissing between his teeth.

She wore only a thin, short-sleeved shirt, a pair of Levi's, and worn-out
Reeboks. The exposed areas of her skin were burned raw, coated with salt
from dried sweat that was as gritty as fine sand; the top of her scalp was
flecked with dried blood from ruptured blisters. A quick inspection revealed
no snake or scorpion bites, no limb fractures or swellings. But she was badly
dehydrated. At somewhere between 15 and 22 percent dehydration a human
being will die, and she had to be close to the danger zone.

Gently he took hold of her shoulders, eased her over onto her back. Her
limbs twitched; she made a little whimpering sound deep in her throat. On
the edge of consciousness, he thought, more submerged than not. The sun's
white glare hurt her eyes through the tightly closed lids. She turned her head,
lifted an arm painfully across the bridge of her nose.

Fallon freed one of the foil-wrapped water bottles, slipped off the attached
cap. Her lips were cracked, split deeply in a couple of places; he dribbled water on them, to get her to open them. Then he eased the spout into her mouth
and squeezed out a few more drops.

At first she struggled, twisting her head, moaning softly now: the part of her that wanted death rebelling against revival and awareness. But her will to live hadn't completely deserted her, and her thirst was too great. She gulped down some of the warm liquid, swallowed more when he lifted her head and held it cushioned against his knee.

Before long she was sucking greedily at the spout, like a baby at its mother's nipple. Her hands came up and clutched at the bottle; he let her take it away from him, let her drain it. The notion of parceling out water to a dehydration victim was a fallacy. You had to saturate the parched tissues as fast as possible to accelerate the restoration of normal functions.

He opened another bottle, raised her into a sitting position, then exchanged it for the empty one in her hands. Shelter was the next most important thing. He took the lightweight space blanket from his pack, unfolded it, and shook it out. Five by seven feet, the blanket was coated on one side with a filler of silver insulating material and reflective surface.

Near where she lay, behind her to the east, he hand-scraped a sandy area free of rocks. Then he set up the blanket into a lean-to, using takedown tent poles to support the front edge and tying them off with nylon cord to rocks placed at forty-five-degree angles from the shelter corners. He secured the ground side of the lean-to with more rocks and sand atop the blanket's edge.

Casey Dunbar was sitting slumped forward when he finished, her head cradled in her hands. The second water bottle, as empty as the first, lay beside her.

Fallon gripped her shoulders again, and this time she stiffened, fought him weakly as he drew her backward and pressed her down into the lean-to's shade. The struggles stopped when he pillowed her head with the pack. She lay unmoving, half on her side, her eyes still squeezed tightly shut. Conscious now, but not ready to face either him or the fact that she was still alive.

The first-aid kit contained a tube of Neosporin. He said as he uncapped it, "I've got some burn medicine here. I'll rub it on your face and scalp first."

She made a throat sound that might have been a protest. But when he squeezed out some of the ointment and began to smooth it over her blistered skin, she remained passive. Lay silent and rigid as he ministered to her.

He used the entire tube of Neosporin, most of it on her face and arms. None of the cuts and abrasions she'd suffered was serious; the medicine would disinfect those, too. There was nothing he could do for the bruises on her upper arms and along her jaw, the scabbed cuts on her left cheek and temple. Those weren't the kind of injuries you got from stumbling around in the desert. They were more than two days old, he judged, already starting to fade. He wondered where she'd gotten them, if somebody had used her for a punching bag.

When he was done, he opened another quart of water, took a nutrition bar from his pack. Casey Dunbar's eyes were open when he looked at her again. Hazel eyes, dull with pain and exhaustion, staring fixedly at him without blinking. Hating him a little, he thought.

He said, "Take some more water," and extended the bottle.

"No."

"Still thirsty, aren't you?"

"No."

"Come on, we both know you are."

"Who're you?" Her voice was as dry and cracked as her lips. "How'd you find me?"

"Richard Fallon—Rick. I was lucky. So are you."

"Lucky," she said.

"Drink the water, Casey."

"How do you know my . . . ? Oh."

"That's right. I read the note."

"Why couldn't you just let me die? Why did you have to come along and find me?"

"Drink."

He held the bottle out close to her face. Her eyes shifted to it; the tip of her tongue flicked out, snakelike, as if she were already tasting the water. Then, grimacing, she raised onto an elbow and took the bottle with an angry, swiping movement—anger directed at herself, he thought, not him, as if she'd committed an act of self-betrayal. She drank almost half before a spasm of coughing forced her to lower the bottle.

"Go a little slower with the rest of it."

"Leave me alone."

"I can't do that, Casey."

"Don't call me that. You don't know me."

"All right."

"I want to sleep," she said.

"No, you don't." He unwrapped the nutrition bar. "Eat as much of this as you can get down. Slowly, little bites."

She shook her head, holding her arms stiff and tight against her sides.

"For your own good."

"I don't want any fucking food."

"Your body needs the nourishment."

"No."

"I'll force-feed you if I have to."

She held out a little longer, but her eyes were on the bar the entire time. When she finally took it, it was with the same gesture of self-loathing. Her first few bites were nibbles, but the honey taste revived her hunger and she went at the bar the way she had at the water bottle, almost choking on the first big chunk she tried to swallow. He made her slow down, sip water after each bite.

"How do you feel now?" he asked when she was finished.

"Like I'm going to live, damn you."

"We'll stay here for a while, until you're strong enough to walk."

"Walk where?"

"My Jeep, over on the trail. Four hundred yards or so, over pretty rough terrain. I don't want to have to carry you the whole way."

"Then what?"

"You need medical attention. There's an infirmary at Furnace Creek Ranch."

"And after that, the psycho ward," she said, but not as if she cared. "Where's the nearest one?"

Fallon let that pass. "If you feel up to talking," he said, "I'm a good listener."

"Talk about what?"

"Why you did this to yourself."

"Tried to kill myself, you mean."

"All right. Why?"

"You read my note."

"Pretty vague. Who's Kevin?"

She turned her head away without answering.

He didn't press her. Instead, he shifted around and lay back on his elbows, with his upper body in the lean-to's shade. He was careful not to touch the woman.

It was another windless day, the near-noon stillness as complete as it had been the other morning in the Funerals. For a time nothing moved anywhere; then a chuckwalla lizard came scurrying up the bank of the wash, followed a few seconds later by a horned toad. It looked as though the toad was chasing the lizard, but like so many things in desert country, that was illusion. Toads and lizards weren't natural enemies.

Before long, Casey stirred and asked if there was any more water. Her tone had changed; resignation flavored it now, as if she'd accepted, at least for the present, the burden of staying alive.

Fallon sat up, removed one of the remaining two full quarts from his pack. "Make this last until we're ready to leave," he said as he handed it to her. "It's a long walk to the Jeep and we'll have to share the last bottle."

She drank less thirstily, lowered the bottle with it still two-thirds full. Good sign. Her body was responding, its movements stronger and giving her less pain.

He let her have another energy bar. She took it without argument, ate it slowly with sips of water. When it was gone, she lifted herself into a sitting position, her head not quite touching the slant of the blanket. She was a few inches over five feet, more sinew than flesh. Her relatively young age, and the kind of body she had and the fact that she'd taken care of it, explained her survival and the relative swiftness of her recovery.

She said, not looking at him, "I guess you might as well know."

"Know what?"

"About Kevin. The rest of it."

"If you want to tell me."

"He's my son. Kevin Andrew Spicer. He's eight and a half years old."

"Court Spicer your husband?"

"Ex-husband, and I hope his soul rots in hell."

"So you hate him. Divorce does that to some people."

"Hate doesn't begin to describe what I feel for him."

"What did he do to you?"

"He took Kevin."

"You mean a custody battle?"

"Oh, yes, but I won that. I had full legal custody of my son."

"Had?"

"Court kidnapped him," Casey said. The words seemed to stick in her throat; she coughed again and swallowed heavily before she went on. "Four months ago, not long after the judgment. He had visitation rights, every other weekend. He picked Kevin up one Friday afternoon and never brought him back."

"Where was this? San Diego?"

"Yes."

"You still live there?"

"I don't live anywhere anymore," she said.

Fallon said, "You must have gone to the authorities."

"The police, the FBI, a private detective I hired—nobody's been able to find them."

"How could they vanish so completely?"

"Money. Everything comes down to money."

"Not everything."

"Court claimed he was broke when I divorced him. All I got was custody and child support that he never paid."

"But he wasn't broke. Hidden assets?"

"I thought so, my lawyer thought so, but we couldn't prove it."

"What does he do for a living?"

"Musician. Second-rate musician."

"Then where'd the hidden assets come from?"

"He had another income, but he wouldn't tell me what it was."

Fallon said, "He must have wanted the boy pretty badly."

"Not because he loves him. He did it to hurt me. He hates me. He can't stand to lose money, property, people, any of his possessions."

"He sounds unstable."

"Unstable is a polite term for it."

"Abusive?" Fallon asked. "You, your son?"

"The verbal kind. His rants caused Kevin to have more than one attack."

"Attack?"

"He's asthmatic. He needs medication . . . if he doesn't get it and he has a serious attack, he could die."

"Spicer wouldn't let that happen, would he?"

"He's capable of it. He's capable of anything, any kind of viciousness."

"Against his own son?"

She didn't answer. She sat stiffly, squinting in the direction of Striped Butte, where the sun threw dazzling glints off its anamorphic conglomeration of limestone and other minerals.

"Banning," Fallon said. "Who's he?"

"The last straw."

He waited, but she didn't go on.

"What happened to your face? You didn't get those cuts and bruises from the desert."

The question made her wince. She said in a dry whisper, "I don't want to talk anymore. My mouth hurts and my throat's sore."

"Drink some more water."

She sucked from the bottle, then lapsed into a brooding silence.

Time passed. Fallon looked up at Manly Peak and the taller, hazy escarpments of Telescope Peak to the north. Some people found the Panamints oppressive. Bare monoliths of dark gray basalt and limestone like tombstones towering above a vast graveyard—mute testimony to the ancient Paiute legend of how they were formed, in an eons-long war among the gods. It was easy enough to imagine them that way, as the earthly remains of cosmic battles in which thunderbolts were hurled like spears, fire was summoned from the earth's core, mountains melted and flowed into the Valley, massive stone blocks were ripped up and flung helter-skelter until they piled so high, new peaks were created.

But there was a stark beauty in them, too. And to Fallon, a sentinel-like quality—old and benevolent guardians, comforting in their size and age and austerity. They held his gaze while he sat there waiting and listening to the silence.

THREE

H E GREW AWARE OF heat rays against his hands where they rested flat
on his thighs. The sun had reached and passed its zenith, was robbing
the shelter of shade. If they didn't leave soon, he would have to reset the
position of the lean-to.

"How do you feel?" he asked Casey. "Strong enough to try walking?"

She was still resigned. "I can try," she said.

"Stay where you are for a couple of minutes, while I get ready. I'll work
around you."

He gathered and stowed the empty water bottles, took down the lean-to
and stowed the stakes, strapped on the pack. When he helped Casey to her
feet, she seemed able to stand all right without leaning on him. Carefully he
put his sun hat on her head, easing it down to cover her sunburned forehead
and scalp. Shook out the blanket, draped it over her head and shoulders so
that her arms were covered, and showed her how to hold it in place under
her chin. Then he slipped an arm around her thin body and they set out.

Long, slow trek to the Jeep. And a painful one for her, though she didn't
complain, didn't speak the entire time. They stayed in the wash most of the
way, despite the fact that it added a third to the distance, because the foot-
ing was easier for her. He stopped frequently so she could rest; and he let
her have most of the remaining water. Still, by the time they reached the
trail her legs were wobbly and most of her new-gained strength was gone.
He had to swing her up and carry her the last hundred yards. Not that it
was much of a strain: she was like a child in his arms.

He eased her into the Jeep's passenger seat, took the blanket, and put it and his pack into the rear. There were two quarts of water left back there. He drank from one, a couple of long swallows, before he leaned in under the wheel. She had slumped down limply in the other seat, with her head back and her eyes shut. Her breath came and went in ragged little pants.

"Casey?"

"I'm awake," she said.

"Here. More water."

She drank without opening her eyes.

He drove back to the Toyota, unlocked the driver's door, opened it carefully because the metal was hot enough raise blisters. He fetched her purse from under the seat, then slid into the stifling interior. Usual junk in the glove compartment; he rummaged through it until he found the registration and an insurance card. He put these into the purse.

When he switched on the ignition, the gas gauge indicator hovered close to empty. He twisted the key to see if the car would start. The engine caught on the third try, stuttering a bit; he shut it off immediately. If the only serious damage was the ruptured oil pan, repairs wouldn't cost much. It was arranging for a tow truck to come out and haul the Camry to the station at Furnace Creek Ranch that would be expensive.

He pulled the trunk release, got out and went around back. Two pieces of luggage in the trunk, a small suitcase and an overnight case. He took these out, closed the lid, locked the car again, and carried purse and luggage back to the Jeep and stowed them in the rear. Casey still slumped low on the seat with her eyes closed. She didn't open them until after they were moving again in the opposite direction and the heated slipstream fanned her face through the open window.

Fallon drove slowly, trying to avoid the worst of the ruts, but a few times as they bounced over the track she gave out low groans. Otherwise she made no complaint, said nothing at all. When they reached the smoother valley road above the Ashford Mill ruins, her breathing grew less labored and he thought she was asleep. If so, the sleep didn't last long. They were halfway between Mormon Point and Badwater when she stirred, shifted position, and drank thirstily from the water bottle. When she lowered it, her pained gaze turned to him.

"How much farther?"

"Forty-five minutes. You okay?"

"Do I look okay? It feels like we've been riding for hours."

"Can I ask you a question?"

"I can't stop you."

"Why did you come here?"

"Where? Where you found me?"

"No, I mean Death Valley. Nearly four hundred miles from San Diego."

"I came from Las Vegas, not San Diego."

"Why were you in Vegas?"

"Fool's errand," she said bitterly.

"Is that where you got those bruises? In Vegas?"

". . . You really want to know?"

"I wouldn't have asked if I didn't."

For a time she was silent. Then abruptly, staring straight ahead, she said in flat tones, "A man called me a few days ago. He said his name was Banning and he knew where Court and Kevin were living, but he wanted two thousand dollars for the information. In cash, delivered to him in Las Vegas."

"Somebody you know, this Banning?"

"No."

"But you believed him."

"I wanted to believe him," Casey said. "He claimed he'd known Court years ago, mentioned the names of people I knew. He said he'd heard that the detective I'd hired had been asking questions about Court."

"Did he say how he'd heard?"

"No. I know I should've asked him, but I didn't."

"What's the detective's name?"

"Sam Ulbrich. He managed to trace Court and Kevin to Las Vegas last week, but that was as far as he got."

"You tell him about Banning's call?"

"No."

"Why not? Why not send him instead of going yourself?"

"He stopped working for me when I couldn't pay him anymore. I had nothing left to sell, nobody to borrow from."

"What about your family?"

"I don't have any family. Except for my son."

"So you couldn't raise the money Banning demanded."

"Oh, I raised it. I went to Vegas with two thousand dollars in my purse."

"Where'd you get it?"

It was several seconds before she answered. Then, in the same flat, lifeless voice, "I stole it."

Fallon didn't say anything.

"I was desperate," she said. "Desperate."

"Stole it where?"

"From the man I work . . . worked for. From the office safe. And I drove to Vegas and gave it to Banning."

"And it was all just a scam," Fallon said. "He didn't know where to find Spicer and your son."

"Oh, he knew, all right. He knew because Court set the whole thing up. That was part of the message Banning delivered afterward."

"Afterward?"

"After he beat me up and raped me."

"Jesus."

"Your ex-husband says you'd better stop trying to find him and Kevin, otherwise there'll be more of the same. Only next time he'll do it himself and it won't just be rape and a beating, he'll kill you. End of message."

"You call the police?"

"What for? Banning isn't his real name. What could the police have done? No. No. I stayed in the motel room where it happened until I felt well enough to leave, and then I started driving. By the time the car quit on me, I was out here in the middle of nowhere and I didn't care anymore. I didn't want to go on living."

"You still feel that way?"

"What do you think?"

Fallon said, "It's a hundred and twenty miles from Vegas to this part of Death Valley. How'd you end up where I found you?"

"I don't know."

"But you did come here intentionally. Death Valley—dead place, place to go and die."

"No. I've never been here before. I told you, I just kept driving until the car stopped. What difference does it make, anyhow?"

"It makes a difference. I think it does."

"Well, I don't. The only thing that matters is that you found me too soon."

They rode in silence again until they reached the intersection with the Shoshone highway. Six miles from there to Furnace Creek Ranch.

He said as much to Casey. "When we get there, I'll tell the infirmary people you made the mistake of driving out into a wilderness area in the wrong kind of vehicle, and when it broke down you tried to walk out and lost your bearings. That sort of thing happens a dozen times a year in the Valley. Nobody will think anything of it."

She was silent.

"After that I'll get a cabin for you so you can rest up."

"Don't you listen? I don't have any money."

"I'll pay for it. You can pay me back later."

"Pay you back how?"

"Cash or check. I don't want anything else from you, Casey."

"Oh, sure. That's what you all say."

"I'm not other men. I'm Rick Fallon."

"Why should Rick Fallon care about me?"

Good question. He kept thinking about the way he'd found her, how she'd looked lying there in the wash. And the suicide note. And everything that she'd told him. And above all the face of the boy, Kevin, smiling at him from the photograph she carried—the boy who looked like Timmy.

But all he said was, "We can talk about that later."

"We've talked enough. I have, anyway. You know my story, so now I'm supposed to listen to yours?"

"No."

"Then we don't have anything left to talk about."

"I think maybe we do," he said, and let it go at that.

FOUR

FURNACE CREEK RANCH WAS a sprawling tourist oasis that Fallon avoided except when he needed to buy gas and supplies. Eighteen-hole golf course, the world's lowest at 214 feet below sea level. Two hundred and twenty-four moderately priced rooms and cabins. Restaurants, saloon and cocktail lounge, shops, a Borax museum, swimming pools fed by underground springs, tennis courts, stables, airstrip, RV and trailer parking, service station. Too crowded, too much engine hum.

It was midafternoon when they drove past the lushly landscaped grounds of the Furnace Creek Inn, just down the road from the Ranch. The Inn catered to those who preferred luxury accommodations and meals at a four-star restaurant. He'd stayed there once with Geena, at her insistence. It had everything you could want—everything she could want, anyway. The engine sounds were more muted there, but he could still hear them, and he missed the silences and wide open freedom of the remote sections of the Valley. He'd never been back to the Inn.

Before he delivered Casey to the infirmary on the palm-shaded Ranch grounds, he repeated the lost-by-accident story he was going to tell and warned her not to say anything to contradict him. Her response was a head bob. She seemed to have lapsed back into a brooding lassitude.

"I'll have to tell it to the park rangers, too," he said. "They may or may not want to talk to you, now or later. If so, just stick to the story."

Another head bob.

There were no problems at the infirmary. The woman on the desk asked for Casey's address and medical insurance card. Casey said she didn't know where her purse was, and Fallon said it was in the Jeep. He went out, checked her wallet and found a Kaiser card. Her driver's license had been issued within the past year, so the address on it—716 Avila Court, San Diego—was probably current. He slipped the license out and took it and the insurance card inside, leaving the purse where it was.

From the infirmary he made his report to the ranger on duty and went from there to the Ranch office. Even though the resort throbbed with people, there was usually space available at this time of year. Today was no exception. He used one of his credit cards to secure a cabin for two nights in the name of C. Dunbar.

At the cabin, he brought her luggage and purse inside and laid them on the bed. Neither bag was locked. With the door shut, he went through them. Nothing but cosmetics and personal hygiene stuff in the overnight bag; no drugs other than a prescription vial of Ambien sleeping tablets. The suitcase contained a skirt, a pair of slacks, a couple of light-colored blouses, a thin poplin jacket, underwear. And wadded up inside one of the liner pockets, a pair of torn cotton panties and a third blouse, white, also torn, and spotted with streaks of dried blood.

He closed both cases and checked the purse again. The name and address on the Toyota's registration was the same as the one on her driver's license. He put that aside and removed the other items one by one. Wallet. Coin purse. Leatherette business-card case. Cell phone. Lipstick, compact, nail clippers, tissues. The last item was a small, round chunk of plaster of paris with the words "For Mom, Love Kevin" etched into it—the kind of thing grade-school kids make and loving parents cherish. Timmy had made something like it for Geena. And for him, a crude wood-modeled keychain that he still carried in his pocket.

He still had Casey's license and insurance card; he returned them to the wallet, then opened the leatherette case. A dozen or so glossy business cards, all done in red and black embossed lettering, all the same: Vernon Young Realty, 14150 Las Palomas Avenue, San Diego. Casey Dunbar, Sales Representative.

The cell phone was charged and working; you could almost always get a satellite signal in this part of the Valley. He opened the cell's address book.

Around a dozen entries, listed by first name or initial or type of business or institution such as "School"; most had telephone numbers only. The few addresses were all in San Diego and environs. The final entry was "S. Ulbrich," with a phone number but no address. He wrote the number down on a sheet of paper from the writing desk.

The wallet next. Other than the one credit card, probably maxed out, and the twelve dollars in cash, there was nothing but the driver's license, medical card, and snapshots of her son. He looked at the snaps again—six of them, ranging from when Kevin was a baby to his present age. The physical resemblance to Timmy was not that strong, really, and yet the boy's image brought memories flooding back. Fallon resisted an urge to take Timmy's photo from his own wallet and compare the two side by side. He closed Casey's wallet and returned it and the rest of the items to her purse.

All right.

Outside he retrieved his cell phone from his pack, took it back into the cabin. The digital clock on the nightstand gave the time as 4:30. Will Rodriguez should still be at Unidyne. He put in a call, waited through a five-minute hold before Will's voice said, "Hey, amigo. I thought you were going packing in Death Valley."

"That's where I am."

"Everything okay?"

"More or less. Listen, Will, are you busy right now?"

"No more than usual. Why?"

"I stumbled into a situation here and I need a favor."

"You got it. What kind of situation?"

"It involves a woman—"

"Ah."

"No, nothing like that," Fallon said. "She's in trouble. I need some information on how bad it is."

"Felony kind?"

"Yes. But I think it might be fixable."

"By you?"

"Depends. Maybe."

"Careful, man. You're pretty vulnerable right now."

"So is she."

". . . Okay. What can I do?"

"Make a couple of phone calls, do an Internet check. You still know people in law enforcement, right?"

"Some. I've been off the job for years, you know that."

"This shouldn't take much effort. The only serious crime involved seems to be parental abduction—not by the woman, by her ex-husband. She apparently had custody of the child."

"What's her name?"

"Casey Dunbar. Seven-sixteen Avila Court, San Diego. Ex-husband is Court Spicer, the kid is Kevin Spicer, age eight and a half. Abduction happened four months ago. She hired a San Diego private detective named Sam Ulbrich and he traced Spicer and the boy to Las Vegas. I'm wondering how reputable he is."

"How do you spell Ulbrich?"

Fallon said, "U-l-b-r-i-c-h," and read off the phone number he'd found in Casey's address book. "One more thing. She did something stupid when she ran out of money. Stole some cash from the real estate outfit where she works to pay off a guy in Vegas who claimed to know where Spicer and the boy were living."

"How much cash?"

"She says two thousand dollars. The company is Vernon Young Realty, 14150 Las Palomas, San Diego."

"And you want to know if theft charges were filed. And if the amount is more than two thousand."

"If she's been straight with me or not. Right."

Will said, "Pretty late in the day. I may not be able to get back to you until tomorrow morning."

"That's soon enough. Call me on my cell. And thanks, Will."

"Por nada. Just remember what I said about being careful. Don't get yourself mixed up in something you'll live to regret."

"I won't forget."

Fallon locked the cabin and drove to the service station, where he reported the location of the Camry and arranged for it to be towed to the Ranch. Then he returned to the infirmary.

The nurse told him Casey was resting, that her burns were relatively minor and her condition not critical. "You did a very good job of hydrating her and tending to her injuries, Mr. Fallon."

"Has she said anything about what happened?"

"No. She didn't want to talk about it."

"About the other injuries? The older ones?"

The nurse's lips pursed. "She said she was in an accident, but it looks to me like she was abused. Do you know anything about that?"

"No. The first time I ever laid eyes on her was in that wash. How long before she's well enough to travel?"

"A day or two, barring infection."

"Can I see her?"

"If she's awake. We gave her a mild sedative."

Casey was asleep. The nurse suggested he come back in two hours; Fallon said he would, and went from there to the saloon. He was tired enough and thirsty enough to crave a cold beer. He sat in a corner with the pint of draft ale, as far from the other customers as he could get, and tuned out bar voices and a TV news broadcast. The same thoughts he'd had on the way in still crowded his mind.

Careful, Rick. You're pretty vulnerable right now. Don't get yourself mixed up in something you'll live to regret.

Good advice, but he had the feeling he was already mixed up in it, already committed. Careful, yes; that was why he'd gone through her things, called Will. But unless it turned out that she'd lied to him about the kidnapping and the stolen money, he couldn't walk away as if he'd never found her. Kevin and the resemblance to Timmy, the abuse she'd suffered, the possibility that she might try to kill herself again . . . they were part of the reason. But there was more, too. He couldn't quite explain it yet, needed to think about it. Not here, though. Someplace where the engines were still and there were no distractions.

The beer made him realize he was hungry. There was a restaurant next to the saloon; he dawdled over a steak sandwich and another draft. Will still hadn't called back by the time he was done. Probably wouldn't until morning.

The two hours were up; he returned to the infirmary. Casey was awake, the nurse told him. He found her groggy but lucid, small and vulnerable on the bed like a wounded child. When he was alone with her he said, "I've got a cabin ready for you. The nurse says I can take you there if you feel up to it. It's just a short ride."

"All right."

"We can get you a wheelchair if you need it."

"No. If I can stand up, I can walk."

He waited five minutes in the anteroom. She came out under her own power, walking slow and stiff but steadily enough. She wouldn't let him help her outside or into the Jeep.

On the way across the grounds he said, "A tow truck will pick up your car tomorrow morning and bring it back here. The mechanics ought to be able to get it running again."

"It doesn't matter. I don't have anywhere to go."

"Maybe you do."

"What does that mean?"

"We'll talk about it tomorrow."

At the cottage she again refused his help, walked inside on her own. When she saw her luggage and purse on the single bed, she gave him a quick sidelong look.

He said, "Don't worry, I won't be staying here. The cabin's all yours."

"You paid for another cabin?"

"No. I prefer sleeping outdoors."

She sat on the edge of the bed. "I can't figure you out."

"Sometimes I can't figure myself out," he said. "I'll come by in the morning, sometime after nine, and we'll talk. You'll still be here?"

"Where am I going to go? I can't pay for the car repairs, either."

FIVE

ALLON SPENT THE NIGHT packed in near Skidoo, the remains of an
old mining camp above Emigrant Canyon. Alone in the stillness, he felt
the tensions of the long day evaporate, his thought processes sharpen until
they were as clear as the crystalline night sky. He knew then the other part
of the reason why he was letting himself become involved in Casey Dunbar's troubles.

The Valley, and his symbiotic relationship to it. As if it was somehow responsible for bringing the two of them together.

He could have gone anywhere within three thousand square miles today,
and yet he'd chosen, or been directed to, the exact spot where the Toyota
had quit running two days ago. He could have easily missed finding her in
the wash, but he hadn't. She could have been dead by then, but she wasn't.
If you looked at it that way, the Valley was just as responsible for saving her
life as he was.

Illusion? False mysticism? Maybe. All he knew for sure was that the con-
cept seemed real to him. If the story Casey had told was essentially factual, he
was obligated to continue watching out for her, to provide her with a reason
to go on living. Otherwise none of today's happenings would mean anything
and his relationship with the Valley would never be quite the same again.

He wondered if he could make her understand this. He wondered if he
should even bother to try. She'd probably think he was crazy. Hell, maybe
he was. But it was a benign form of lunacy, the kind that allowed a man to
live at peace with himself.

At first light he went for a five-mile roundabout hike that eventually brought him back to the Jeep. By then the day's heat was just beginning to seep through the night chill. He drove out of the canyon to Stovepipe Wells, a smaller food and lodging settlement on the desert flats; filled the Jeep's gas tank and then went into the restaurant for coffee and a plate of eggs and toast.

Will Rodriguez called as he was about to start the thirty-mile drive to Furnace Creek Ranch. "Sorry I didn't get back to you yesterday, amigo. I couldn't get hold of a couple of people until this morning."

"What did you find out?"

"The woman seems to've told you a straight story. She brought a legitimate kidnapping charge against her ex-husband four months ago. Still outstanding. He and the kid have dropped completely off the radar."

"What about the theft charge against her?"

"There isn't one," Will said. "No warrant of any kind."

"Sure?"

"Positive."

"So Vernon Young didn't file a complaint after all."

"Why wouldn't he? Two thousand bucks is two thousand bucks."

"He may not know yet that the money is missing. Or if he knows why she took it, maybe he feels sorry for her."

"Or she has some reason to lie to you about the theft."

"She have any history with the law I should know about?"

"No. Clean slate."

"The husband, Court Spicer?"

"Court short for Courtney. He's another story. Three arrests, one for aggravated assault—bar fight—and two for drunk and disorderly. The most recent D&D was six months ago, right before the custody hearing. One reason why the judge ruled against him, probably."

"Casey told me he hid assets before the divorce, that that's how he financed his disappearing act."

"Could be, but it didn't come from his job."

"Musician, right?"

"Right. Piano player—solo lounge jobs or with small jazz groups."

"What'd you find out about the detective, Sam Ulbrich?"

"Operates in San Diego under the name Confidential Investigative Services," Will said. "Former police officer like most, in business for himself about fifteen years. Brought up before the Department of Consumer Affairs five years ago for overcharging a client. He claimed it was bogus; the judge agreed and his license wasn't suspended. Otherwise, he seems to have a decent rep."

"Okay. Anything else I should know?"

"That's the whole package. So what're you going to do?"

"About Casey Dunbar? I'm not sure yet. Depends on her."

"Well, whatever you do, just don't all of a sudden drop off the radar yourself."

Casey was waiting for him in her cabin, with the air conditioner cranked all the way up to near chilly. Dressed in clean clothes, her hair washed and brushed, her sun-blotched face and arms greasy with burn ointment. The deep cracks in her lips had already begun to scab over.

"Feeling better this morning?" he asked.

"I suppose so." She seemed to mean it; the dull, hopeless look had faded. Not exactly glad to be alive, he thought, but no longer wishing she weren't.

"Had breakfast?"

"No. I didn't want to go out looking like this."

"You can get room service here."

"On your money? No, thanks."

"You need to eat," Fallon said. He went to the phone, put in an order for a light breakfast without consulting her about the contents.

"You're pushy as hell, aren't you?" she said when he hung up. There was spirit in the words, but no rancor. She wasn't angry at him, but at herself and what she saw as the hopelessness of her situation.

"Sometimes. When I need to be."

"How long are you going to keep it up? All this Good Samaritan stuff."

"As long as you'll let me."

"What would your wife say if she knew?"

"I'm not married. Not anymore."

"So you say."

"I can prove it to you, if it'll make you feel better."

"Okay, so you're unattached and full of the milk of human kindness. And you expect me to believe there's nothing in all this for you?"

"There's something in it for me."

"Uh-huh. Now we get to the bottom line."

"The bottom line," Fallon said, "is I might be able to help you find your son."

The hazel eyes widened. "What're you talking about?"

"Just what I said. Find your son, get him back to you."

". . . You can't be serious."

"Never more serious."

"My God. Then you must be out of your mind. Weren't you listening when I told you about the money I stole?"

"I was listening. You're not wanted by the police, Casey. Vernon Young hasn't filed theft charges against you."

"He . . . how do you know his name?"

"Does it matter?"

Reflexive headshake. "Are you sure he hasn't filed charges?"

"I'm sure."

She bit her lower lip, grimaced because her teeth caught one of the scabbed places.

"If he knows the money is missing," Fallon said, "he understands why you took it. He may be waiting to hear from you, hoping you'll decide to pay it back. It's only been a few days. Grace period."

"But I don't have it, I can't pay it back."

"Not right away. Arrangements can be made."

"What do you mean, arrangements?"

"Monthly payments. Or if necessary, a loan to pay it back all at once."

"Nobody would loan me that much money."

"I might," he said, to see what she'd say.

"What are you . . . oh, come on. Two thousand dollars?"

"I can afford it."

"No. I wouldn't feel right accepting that much money from you."

"We could have a legal paper drawn up and notarized."

"How do you know you could trust me?"

"I don't."

"Oh, but you'd be willing to take the risk."

"Maybe. If it comes down to that."

"If you think it would get me into bed with you—"

"Oh, Christ. What kind of man would I be if I expected that, after all you've been through?"

"I don't know what kind of man you are, not really."

"I'll say this one last time: I don't want *anything* from you."

"Right." Edge of sarcasm in her voice now. "You saved my life, a stranger, and now you're willing to loan me two thousand dollars and help me find my son. That doesn't make any sense."

"It does to me."

"What can you do? You're not a detective—" She broke off, blinked, and said, "Or are you?"

"In a way. I work for a big pharmaceutical company in L.A.—assistant to the head of security. That gives me resources. It's how I found out that no theft charges had been filed."

"Checking up on me."

"Does that bother you?"

"No. But . . . finding people? Do you know how to do that? The police, the FBI couldn't find Kevin. Neither could the detective I hired."

"Maybe none of them tried hard enough. Or looked in the right places."

She kept on staring at him. "I don't know what to think," she said. "I'm not used to dealing with somebody like you. Most of the people I've known in my life are takers, not givers."

"Like your ex-husband."

"Yes. Exactly. Court . . . you don't know him. He meant what he said about killing me. He'd kill you too, if you got in his way."

"I'm not afraid of men like Court Spicer. He may be off the rails, but he's also a coward. Sending Banning after you proves that."

"But you'd still be risking your life for a stranger, two strangers. Saint Rick? I don't believe that."

"My soon-to-be ex-wife said I used to be a fighter, somebody who welcomed challenges, but that I'm not that way anymore. I think she was wrong."

"Meaning you want to prove her wrong."

"It's not like that."

"How is it, then?"

"The split wasn't ugly like yours. I don't have anything to prove to her."

"To yourself, then?"

He shrugged. "There are other reasons. Some you'd understand, some you might not."

"That's an evasive answer."

"All right. I'll tell you the main one." Fallon opened his wallet, removed the snapshot of Timmy from its glassine pocket, handed it to her. "My son. Timothy James Fallon."

She said, staring at it, "He . . . looks like Kevin."

"He would've been the same age."

"Would've been?"

"He died," Fallon said. "Three years ago."

He thought he saw the shape of her expression change. She sat motionless, looking at the photo. "How?"

"An accident. A stupid accident. He climbed a tree with some other kids on a dare, lost his balance, hit the ground on the back of his head. Inoperable brain damage. He was in a coma for three weeks before he died."

"God."

"I was at work when it happened," he said. "There wasn't anything I could do to save him. Maybe there's something I can do to save your son. Do you want me to try?"

She sat holding the snapshot of Timmy, alternating her gaze between it and Fallon. Making a decision.

"Yes," she said at length. "I want you to try."

SIX

WHILE CASEY ATE HER room-service meal, he quizzed her about her ex-husband, her son, and the man who called himself Banning.

Court Spicer first. Fallon asked for his description, since she had no photograph to give him. Average height. Lean and wiry, about 160 pounds. Black curly hair that he wore long, so long the last time she'd seen him that he'd had it in a ponytail. Clean-shaven then. Blue-gray eyes, very intense. Long-fingered hands. Mole on his left cheek, near his mouth. "I used to think he was good-looking. Now," she said bitterly, "I think I must have been out of my mind."

Nothing much there, except maybe for the mole. Mr. Average. And weight can be gained, hair cut and dyed, beards or mustaches grown, a man's appearance changed in a dozen other ways.

"Tell me about your relationship with him," Fallon said. "Start with how you met."

Talking about Spicer was difficult for her. She spoke haltingly, her gaze slanted off much of the time in a fixed stare. She'd gone with a friend to a small club in San Diego's Old Town district, she said, where Spicer had been playing piano. He'd noticed her, kept looking at her and smiling, and on his break he'd gone to their table for introductions, bought a round of drinks. She was flattered by the attention, but not attracted to him enough to say yes when he asked her for a date.

Two days later he'd surprised her with a phone call. She hadn't given him her home number; he'd gotten it some other way. The persistent type. She was lonely enough to agree then to have drinks with him.

That casual date led to others. He didn't try to talk her into sleeping with him. Kept it low-key. He could be charming, she said. Amusing, fun to be with. He took her to good restaurants, shows, jazz clubs, and improv sessions where he sat in from time to time—a whole new world for her.

She'd been seeing him off and on for three months when he proposed. She said no, but she kept on dating him, and he kept on asking her, and one night, after too much to drink, she let him take her to bed. The next morning he asked her again and she said yes. They were married in City Hall two weeks later.

"It wasn't a bad marriage at first," she said. "He could be moody sometimes, but mostly he was sweet to me. But that all changed when I made a mistake with my birth-control pills and got pregnant."

"How'd he take the news?"

"He just . . . blew up. He didn't want kids, not right away. He was so furious, I thought he was going to hit me. That was the first time I saw the other side of him . . . the first time I was afraid of him."

Spicer wanted her to have an abortion. She refused. They fought about it and when she wouldn't give in, the marriage turned rocky. He joined a trio that played road gigs, keeping him away from home for several weeks at a time. When he came back to San Diego, he spent little time at home with her. He was gone somewhere the night her water broke. She had to call for an EMS ambulance to take her to the hospital.

She'd come close to divorcing him at that point. But when he finally showed up at the hospital he'd been apologetic and full of promises; fawned over his new son. So she'd stayed with him, more for Kevin's sake than her own.

For six years Spicer more or less lived up to his role as husband, father, and family provider. He worked steadily, mostly in the San Diego area, though the money he made combined with her modest income was barely enough to pay the bills. When Kevin was six months old, Casey had found a woman to take care of him during the day for a reasonable fee and gone back to work for Vernon Young Realty, the sales rep job she'd had when she met Spicer. It was the only way, she said, that they could make ends meet.

What finally sent the marriage skidding downhill was Spicer's professional failures and frustrations. Better gigs eluded him; every tryout with a topflight band failed. And no one in the profession liked the elaborate piano compositions and band arrangements he wrote. He grew more and more moody and depressed. Lost his temper at the slightest provocation, threw screaming fits. Accused Casey of having affairs with neighbors, coworkers, strangers. Began drinking heavily, staying away from home for days at a time without explanation. Lost or quit one job after another.

Then, three years ago, things had gotten better for a time. Spicer's whole attitude changed after his return from a road trip, became upbeat, cheerful. Their financial troubles were over, he told her, and proved it by paying off some of their debts and buying her and the boy presents. He claimed to have found a new, well-paying gig at the Beach Club in La Jolla, to have sold one of his jazz compositions to a large recording company. But he wouldn't let her go with him to La Jolla to hear him play, and he was evasive when she asked who'd bought the composition.

She grew suspicious enough to drive to La Jolla alone one night. He wasn't at the Beach Club; the management had never heard of him. In their apartment she went through his desk looking for, and not finding, a copy of the recording company contract he claimed to have signed. She confronted him the next day. He flew into a rage, refusing to explain why he'd lied to her or where the extra money was coming from. Warned her not to meddle in his private business.

"You don't have any idea how much he had or was getting?" Fallon asked.

"No, but it had to be a lot from the way he was spending at first. Thousands."

"More coming in over a period of time?"

"Yes. I think so."

Spicer's mystery income wasn't enough to keep him happy. Not long after the confrontation he underwent another change, back to his Hyde persona with a vengeance. Long absences, verbal abuse when he was home, more heavy drinking, and the bar fight that led to his arrest for aggravated assault. Finally she'd had enough. Told him she wanted a divorce. He shoved her, threw her down on the couch—the closest he'd come to physical violence.

Accused her of leaving him for another man. Threatened to "make her pay" if she went through with the divorce.

"That was the last straw," she said. "I just couldn't take it anymore. I hired a lawyer and took Kevin and moved out. He found out the new address and kept calling up at all hours, drunk or stoned and yelling obscenities. Then he got his own lawyer and sued for custody. Spite and hate, that's all it was. He doesn't give a damn about Kevin.

"I had no trouble getting the divorce, but the custody trial dragged on and on. Court put on a good show, the loving, misunderstood father, all that crap. The judge saw through it and gave me full custody."

"What was Spicer's reaction?"

"None at first. He didn't make a scene or bother me afterward. But he had visitation rights, one weekend a month—there wasn't anything I could do about that. The first few weekends, he brought Kevin home when he was supposed to. Then the last time he didn't. He'd packed up and left, without a word to the landlord or anybody else. The police found his car later, abandoned, in El Cajon. If he bought another one, he must have done it under a different name."

"Or had someone buy it for him," Fallon said. "What about his friends?"

"He didn't have any, at least none that I knew about. Just casual acquaintances, almost all of them musicians." She paused and then said, "Eddie Sparrow."

"Who's he?"

"A trumpet player Court worked with once. That's how Sam Ulbrich managed to trace Court to Las Vegas—Eddie Sparrow."

Ulbrich had found out that Sparrow was playing with a jazz band at a club off the Vegas Strip, and gone there to interview him. Sparrow told him he'd run into Spicer at a private jam session the weekend before last, but hadn't talked to him and didn't know where he was living.

Fallon asked, "The club where Sparrow's working—what's it called?"

It took her a little time, but she dredged the name out of her memory. The Hot Licks Club.

"All right. Can you think of anyone Spicer might know in Vegas besides Eddie Sparrow?"

"No."

"Did he ever take you to Vegas?"

"No."

"Go there by himself?"

"The trio he was with had a four-week gig there once."

"When was that?"

"A few years ago." She paused. "You know, it was right before he came into all that extra money."

"So the money may have come from some source in Vegas. Did he go back there after that?"

"Not that I know of."

"Did Ulbrich check with the musicians' union to find out if Spicer's working there now?"

"Yes. Court's union card is still valid, but they wouldn't give out any information about him."

Fallon said, "Okay. Now tell me about Kevin."

"Tell you what? Except for his asthma, he's just a normal boy."

"How bad is the asthma? Does he need to see a specialist?"

"No. Any doctor can prescribe his medication."

"How do you think he reacted to being taken by his father?"

"Scared and bewildered. How else?"

"Would he try to run away if he had the chance?"

"No."

"You sound pretty sure of that."

"He's always been cowed by Court. Afraid of him. If he tried to run and Court caught him . . . No, he wouldn't do that."

Fallon asked about the boy's interests. Sports, outdoor activities?

"Well, he's not good at team games. He's quiet, shy, he doesn't make friends easily. He'd rather read fantasy books like *The Hobbit* and play video games than anything else."

"Good with computers?"

"Like all kids these days. But Court knows that. He wouldn't let Kevin near a computer by himself."

Fallon nodded. He let a few seconds pass before he said, "This isn't going to be easy for you, but now I need to know about Banning."

Her eyes slanted away again; he could see her steeling herself.

"You're sure you never saw him before that day in the motel?"

"Positive," she said.

"Never heard his voice before?"

"No. It was deep, growly . . . I'd remember if I had."

"What exactly did he say to you on the phone?"

"He'd heard that I was looking for my son and ex-husband, that he knew Court and knew where they were living and he'd tell me for two thousand dollars. Bring the money to Las Vegas and he'd meet me and when I paid him, he'd tell me where to find them."

"Did he say how he knew Spicer?"

"He said he'd tell me when he saw me."

"Did he use Sam Ulbrich's name?"

"No. Why should he?"

"No reason, unless he got your number from Ulbrich."

". . . Are you saying Sam Ulbrich helped set me up?"

"I don't know Sam Ulbrich."

"Neither did I, before I hired him. I picked his name out of the phone book. His office isn't far from where I live."

"He didn't have to know you or Spicer to set you up," Fallon said. "Detectives can be bought off during the course of an investigation."

"I don't believe it. He was very professional, he didn't try to overcharge me or anything like that. For God's sake, Court isn't that powerful. He doesn't have unlimited funds, he can't corrupt everybody."

"So we'll assume Ulbrich's clean. Let's get back to Banning. You agreed to his terms, and he told you when and where to meet him."

"The Rest-a-While Motel, room twenty, at three o'clock Wednesday afternoon."

Fallon asked where the motel was located. North Las Vegas, she said, on North Rancho Drive. She didn't remember the exact address. Small, old, nondescript—the cut-rate type of place.

"Was the room reserved in your name?"

"No, Banning said I was to check in and wait for him in number twenty. But I think the clerk may have been expecting me."

"Oh?"

"I didn't have to ask for room twenty. As soon as he saw my name on the registration card, he gave me the key."

He asked if she'd gotten the clerk's name. She hadn't. But she remembered the man well enough: midforties, balding, slightly built but with a noticeable paunch.

"How long were you in the room before Banning showed up?"

"About ten minutes."

So he'd either had surveillance on the motel, so he knew when she arrived, or he'd got a call from the clerk. He'd been somewhere close by, in any case.

"Describe him."

After a few seconds she said, "Not handsome, not ugly. About your height, six feet. Heavyset but not fat. Strong. I couldn't fight him. I couldn't even scream with his hand on my throat. He—"

"Don't dwell on that. How old?"

"Thirties. Maybe thirty-five."

"Hair color?"

"Black. Short and kinky."

"Distinguishing marks? Scars, moles, anything like that."

"A tattoo. On the back of his right wrist."

"What kind of tattoo?"

"A dragon. Breathing fire."

"What was he wearing?"

"Brown leather jacket. Slacks, shirt, cowboy boots . . ." She paused, frowning. "He had something odd in the jacket pocket. It fell out when he took the jacket off and he grabbed it and stuffed it back—quick, as if he didn't want me to see it."

"Did you get a good look at it?"

"No, but I'm pretty sure it was a garter. Gold, with black ruffles around the edge. I think it had writing on it."

"Writing?"

"A name of some kind."

Not a woman's garter, then. A sleeve garter. Some casino employees— floor bosses, dealers, croupiers, stickmen, bartenders—wore them. The name on it could be that of a casino.

"Can you remember anything else about him?"

"He wore a ring, a big gold cat's-eye ring. One of the times he hit me, it cut my cheek."

"You're doing fine," Fallon said. "Now, what about his car?"

"I didn't see it. I didn't even hear him drive up."

"Okay. What did he say to you when you let him in?"

"Just . . . 'I'm Banning.' He was smiling."

"And then?"

"He asked if I'd brought the money and I said yes and took it out of my purse and gave it to him. He counted it before he put it in his pocket. Then . . . then his smile changed and he said, 'All right, now you get what's coming to you,' and that's when he grabbed me and threw me down on the bed. It all happened so fast . . ."

"When did he deliver the warning? While he was attacking you?"

"No. After he . . . afterwards."

"Can you remember his exact words?"

She'd picked up her coffee cup; the question made her put it down again, hard, so that it rattled the saucer and nearly tipped over. "I'll never forget it. 'Message from your ex-husband. Stop looking for him and the kid. If you don't, he'll find you and do what I just did to you and then he'll kill you. And if you go to the police, I'll find you and fuck you again and then *I'll* kill you.'"

"That all?"

"Isn't it enough?"

She had begun to rock slightly, back and forth. There were goose bumps, he saw, rising on her bare arms. The conversation, the chilly air in the room, physiological reaction to the sunburns.

He said, "That's enough for now. You'd better lie down for a while, get some rest."

"I'm all right."

"No, you're not. Not yet."

He got up to turn the air-conditioning unit down to medium cool. She wouldn't let him help her to the bed. When she was lying down with a sheet over her lower body, she said, "What are you going to do now?"

"Go see about your car. It should've been towed in by this time and if it's not too badly damaged, the mechanics ought to have it ready to drive by tomorrow. You won't be ready to travel before then anyway. Probably not until Monday."

"I can't just sit around in this cabin for two more days . . ."

"You will if you want my help." He went to the writing desk, found a piece of cheap motel stationery and a pen. "What's your cell phone number?"

She gave it to him and he wrote it down. Then he tore the paper across the middle, pocketed the top half, and on the clean bottom portion wrote his cell number. He put that piece on the nightstand.

"Call me if you need to at any time. Otherwise I'll call you."

"From where? Where are you going?"

Fallon smiled wryly. "The other side of silence."

"What?"

"Vegas," he said, "where else?"

PART II
LAS VEGAS

ONE

FALLON HAD ALWAYS THOUGHT of Vegas as a massive, amoeba-like creature slowly inching its way across the flat desert landscape, absorbing more and more of it in little nibbling bites. No head or tail, no intelligence, its only purpose to grow larger, fatter, like the others of its kind that had covered the Los Angeles basin and the Phoenix area and were now swallowing parts of the Mojave Desert. Its veins and arteries pulsed and glowed, new cells made up of housing developments and strip malls and big-box stores expanded in every direction as it grew. Heat radiated from it, but it wasn't the dry, natural heat of Death Valley. It was sweaty, oily, carbonized. Body heat. Engine heat.

Worst of all was the noise it generated. Growls, snarls, howls, roars, siren shrieks, and all the other sounds that came from its writhing bowels in a throbbing, never-ending din. There were louder assaults on the eardrums—NASA rocket launches, supersonic jets on takeoffs and flyovers—but they didn't go on and on and on. Only two places were worse than the city beasts. One was a military training base during ongoing preparations for war. The other was war itself, the deadly thunder of bombs and rockets, grenades and small-arms fire—hellsounds that by pure chance he had never had to endure himself.

This creature, the Vegas creature, seemed to be spreading even faster than he recalled. Only five years since he'd been there last, on a concessional week-end with Geena, but it might've been decades. Accelerated metabolism, increased hunger: proportionately less desert. One of the fastest-growing cities in America. One of the fastest-dying open spaces in the West.

Geena loved it, of course. Not so much Vegas itself as its pulsing, pounding heart—the Strip. The skyscraping, weirdly shaped casinos like New York, New York, Bellagio, Bally's, Luxor, the Venetian; the lounge acts and musical extravaganzas; the eye-stabbing neon colors that obscured the night sky—all the gaudy, tawdry, money-driven glitz the City Where Anything Goes could supply. To her it was the epitome of excitement. Worked on her like an aphrodisiac, he remembered. Their sex life had never been as lush and experimental as it had been on their few short stays in Vegas.

He couldn't help wondering briefly, as he reached the northern outskirts, if she'd been here yet with the new man in her life. His name was Macklin—a gynecologist, of all things. Good practice, plenty of money to give her the material possessions she craved. That was all Fallon knew or cared about Macklin or Geena's affair with him or their future prospects together. You love someone, you live together and suffer and grieve together, and then you fall out of love and drift apart and move on. Happens all the time. Doesn't have to be bitter or adversarial. All it really has to be is final.

He didn't need a map to find the Rest-a-While Motel. The Jeep's GPS navigator took care of that. North Rancho Drive was off Highway 93 in North Las Vegas, a few miles from the old downtown. It took him longer to get there crosstown from Highway 95 than the GPS estimate because of heavy Saturday afternoon traffic, like bunched-together platelets clogging the creature's arteries.

Casey had described the motel as nondescript and cut-rate. Right. It took up most of a block between a Denny's and a strip mall, in a section of small businesses and fast-food joints and discount wedding chapels. Low parallel wings stretched vertically from the street, ten units in each, facing one another across an area of dried-out grass that contained a swimming pool and lanai area. The desert sun had baked a brownish tinge into its off-white paint job. A sign jutting skyward in front claimed that it had Las Vegas's most inexpensive rates, free HBO. A small sign said VACANCY.

Either the Denny's parking lot or the strip mall would have been a good place to watch and wait for an expected arrival; easy, then, to walk or drive over to the motel. Number twenty would be one of the rear units, farthest from the street, probably in the wing that backed up against the fenced side yard of an auto-body shop. If the rooms closest to it had been vacant, the sounds of a woman being beaten and raped, even in broad daylight, wouldn't have carried far or alerted anybody. And Banning, the son of a bitch, had been careful, methodical in his assault: hand around Casey's throat, panting threats in her ear to stifle her cries.

Fallon went inside the office. Small, but not too small to hold a bank of slot machines and a TV turned on to a sports channel. A chattery air conditioner vied with the voices from a row of talking heads. Behind the short counter, a man wearing a Hawaiian-style shirt had been perched on a stool staring at the talking heads; he stood up when Fallon came in. Middle-aged, slightly built with a noticeable paunch and an advanced case of male-pattern baldness. He pasted on a smile as Fallon stepped up to the counter.

"Help you, sir?"

"I'm looking for a friend of mine."

"One of our guests?"

"Probably not. But maybe you know him. Calls himself Banning."

The clerk's expression was as flat as a concrete wall. "Doesn't sound familiar."

"Big, heavyset, tattoo of a fire-breathing dragon on his right wrist."

"No. Sorry."

"You work every day this week?" Fallon asked.

"Since Tuesday."

"Here on the desk every afternoon about this time?"

"That's right. Why?"

"Then you remember a young blonde woman, Casey Dunbar, who checked in around three o'clock on Wednesday."

Flicker of something in the man's eyes. They slanted away from Fallon's, to a point above his right ear. "I see a lot of faces every day. Can't remember them all."

"You gave her number twenty. She didn't stay long, not much more than an hour."

"None of my business how long they stay."

"Banning showed up right after she did, paid her a visit. He didn't stay long either."

"So? What're you getting at?"

"The maid report anything out of the ordinary when she cleaned up afterward?"

"Such as what?"

"Such as bloodstains on the sheets."

"Bloodstains?" Now there was a little twitch under the clerk's eye, like a piece of the concrete wall that had worked itself loose. It took him a couple of seconds to smooth it down again. "Listen, Mister—"

"*Did* the maid report anything like that?"

"No. What's the idea of all these questions? You're not a cop or you'd have proved it by now."

"Let's just say I'm a friend of Casey Dunbar's."

"Yeah, well, I don't know anything about her or this guy Banning or any bloodstains Wednesday afternoon. You satisfied now?"

"Let me have a room for the night," Fallon said. "Number twenty."

The clerk was going to refuse; his mouth started to shape the words. But the way Fallon was looking at him changed his mind. "I don't want any trouble here," he said.

"Just a room. Twenty's free, isn't it?"

". . . Yeah, it's free."

"How much?"

"Only one night?"

"That's what I said. How much?"

"Like the sign says—forty-nine ninety-five."

He took his time producing a registration card, sliding it across the counter. Fallon filled it out, transposing two of the numbers on the Jeep's license plate. The name he printed on the card was in block letters, easy enough to read upside down.

The clerk read it aloud: "Court Spicer." The name didn't seem to mean anything to him.

Fallon laid three twenties on the counter, waited for his change and the room key. Still no eye contact. And no more words except for a by-rote, "Check-out time's eleven A.M."

A gamble, playing it this way. If the clerk knew Banning and reported to him, it might flush him out into the open—potentially a quicker way to make contact than trying to track him down on skimpy information. Potentially dangerous, too, but what Fallon had told Casey was true: he wasn't afraid of men who beat up and raped and extorted money from women. The bigger risk was that if Spicer was still in Vegas, Banning would report to him and he'd spook and take Kevin somewhere else.

A gamble, sure. But this was a gambler's town, and there was risk no matter what game you played.

Fallon drove to the rear and parked in the space in front of number 20, the last in the row on the far side as he'd guessed. He took his pack in with him. Not much of a room: bed, nightstand, dresser, one scarred naugahyde chair, TV bolted to an iron swivel, tiny bathroom with a stall shower. Stifling in there, the smell of Lysol disinfectant nearly overpowering; the room likely hadn't been rented since Wednesday. You'd need a UV fluorescein detector to find the blood traces in here now.

He put the air conditioner on low, drew the drapes over the single window, made sure the door was locked. Then he sat on the lumpy bed, opened the phone book he found in a nightstand drawer. The Hot Licks Club and Casino was on Flamingo, probably in a section close to the Strip.

He debated calling Vernon Young in San Diego. Casey didn't want Fallon to bail her out, but he didn't see any reason to wait before getting in touch with her boss. The quicker the money issue was resolved, the better it would be for her. And if resolving it meant loaning her the two thousand, all right—another gamble. But he doubted it would come to that.

AT&T Information gave him the number of Vernon Young Realty. He put in the call, but Vernon Young wasn't there. The woman who answered said he didn't come in on weekends. Fallon persuaded her to give out his home number by saying, "It's important that I talk to him. It has to do with some money he's owed." But when he called the home number, an answering machine picked up. He didn't leave a message.

Fallon hauled his pack onto the bed, unzipped the side pocket where he kept his handgun in its supple leather holster. Ruger .357 Magnum revolver, four-inch barrel. Moderately heavy piece at two and a half pounds. More weapon than he needed for his routine security job at Unidyne and for self-defense against snakes on his desert treks, but he was comfortable with it. The army had taught him to shoot, and he'd been comfortable with the heavier military sidearms. Ranked high in marksmanship in basic training at Fort

Benning—good hand-eye coordination, steady aim, easy trigger pull. That was one of the reasons they'd assigned him to MP duty instead of letting him train in electronics as he'd requested. A matter of aptitude, he was told.

He hadn't much liked the MP duty at first. Mainly it involved routine patrols and handling drunken noncoms and issuing citations. Good at it, though, because he'd applied himself, and somebody at the command level had decided that was where he belonged. He'd spent his entire four-year tour at two stateside bases, Fort Benning and Fort Huachuca. Never left U.S. soil the entire time. Fort Huachuca was the better of the two duties by far because it was in Cochise County, in the southeastern part of Arizona— desert country, the place where he'd first learned that deserts were so much more than arid wastelands.

Everybody always said he was lucky. Not only because of the easy state-side duty, but because his tour had fallen between the times of intense foreign combat—enlisted in '93 at age eighteen, after Desert Storm, and discharged in '97 before Nine-Eleven, Afghanistan, Iraq. Maybe he *was* lucky. Like every other soldier he'd ever known, he'd had no desire to get his ass shot off. And yet he'd come close to reenlisting after the Nine-Eleven terrorist attack in New York City. Would have, if Geena hadn't talked him out of it for Timmy's sake.

Geena. Timmy. A whole different life back then.

The Ruger was unloaded; he kept it that way whenever he was in Death Valley, except when he was packing well off the beaten track, because loaded firearms are illegal in national parks. Rattlesnakes aren't, though, and self-defense was more important than strictly following rules. He swung the gate open, looked at the empty chambers for several seconds, and then closed the gate again and sat holding the weapon in his hand. He'd never fired it anywhere except at the police range, once every other month in competitions with Will Rodriguez that he usually won. Never had occasion to draw it even once in the nine years he'd been with Unidyne. Never drawn it in the wilderness, either. He'd seen his share of sidewinders, but never been surprised by one up close.

He could and would shoot a man if he had to. Army training: if your weapon was loaded and you had reason to draw it, you had to be prepared to fire. But only in self-defense. He'd thrown down on fellow soldiers twice dur-

ing his MP days, one of them a kid from Tennessee on a violent meth high
who was threatening bar patrons with a bayonet. He would've fired a kill shot
when the kid started to attack him, if his partner hadn't swung a blindside
billy first. The incident had made Fallon think what it would be like to shoot
an assailant, shoulder the responsibility for a man's death. He didn't like the
idea, but he didn't shy away from it either. Putting yourself into a potentially
deadly situation meant being willing to do what you had to do to protect
yourself. True as an MP and corporate security officer, true as a civilian.

But he was on thin ice here. His California carry permit was no good in
Nevada or any other state, and the gun laws here in Vegas were strict. O. J.
Simpson and his buddies had found that out the hard way. He could keep the
weapon in his pack, but to be strictly legal it would have to be unloaded. An
empty sidearm was worthless except as a bluff threat, and if the bluff were
called with a loaded piece, you could end up dead.

So the smart thing to do was not to rely on ordnance at all. Keep the
Ruger unloaded and tucked away. He was a big man, strong, he was skilled
in hand to hand combat methods, he could handle himself against men
like Banning and Court Spicer. Sure he could—as long as they weren't
armed with chambered weapons and likewise prepared to use them.

He asked himself, not for the first time and not for long, if he'd bitten
off more than he could chew. Could be. But he was already committed.
And the doubts dissolved when he thought about what Banning and Spicer
had done to Casey, the probably frightened eight-and-a-half-year-old with
asthma, the promises he'd made. He'd see it through, one way or another.

The digital clock on the nightstand read 4:33. Lull time in the clubs and
casinos, especially on a Saturday. If Eddie Sparrow was still playing at the
Hot Licks Club, it wasn't likely he'd be there until evening. Making the
rounds to find out which if any of the casinos used gold and black-ruffled
sleeve garters could wait a while, too.

He put the unloaded Ruger away, lowered the pack to the floor, then lay
back on the bed. The air conditioner made a clunky humming noise. Outside, kid cries from the pool and traffic noise on North Rancho Drive filtered in faintly.

The kid cries started him thinking about Timmy again. He took out the
good, cherished memories as he often did, let them stream like slides across

his mind. The boy's love of baseball and their backyard pitch-and-catch games and the trips to Dodger Stadium. The time they'd gone camping together in the Mojave, just the two of them, and how excited Timmy had been. Their first visit to Death Valley, Geena with them that time, and the wonder in the boy's eyes as he gazed out at the changing colors of the hills from atop Zabriskie Point. The other places they'd gone and the other things they'd done, and the sound of Timmy's laughter at cartoon antics and silly kid jokes.

The slide show ended abruptly, as it always did, with the image of a still, pale, bandaged face in a white room, the last image before the middle-of-the-night call from the hospital and the doctor's solemn voice saying, "I'm afraid I have some bad news for you, Mr. Fallon."

Timmy.

Ah, God—Timmy.

For an hour Fallon lay motionless, waiting, trying not to think about anything once the memories were locked away again. The army, with its hurry-up-and-wait philosophy, had taught him the rudiments of patience; the routine at Unidyne and the desert treks had honed and refined it for him.

The phone didn't ring. No one knocked on the door.

That didn't mean anything one way or another. He was pretty sure the desk clerk knew the man who called himself Banning, had some idea of what had gone on in this room on Wednesday, and had been paid for his collusion and his silence. If that was the way things shaped up, the clerk would report to Banning. What Banning did about it, if anything, was a matter of wait-and-see.

At 5:30 Fallon tried Vernon Young's home number a second time, got the answering machine again. He called Casey's cell, to find out how she was doing. There seemed to be some life in her voice when she said she was all right, feeling better. He told her he was in Vegas, but not where he was staying the night, and a little of what he was planning for tonight. There wasn't much else to say except that he'd call again in the morning.

*   *   *

Six o'clock.

No calls, no visitors.

Fallon went into the bathroom for a small strip of toilet paper. Outside, with the pack slung over his shoulder, he closed the toilet paper into the joining of the door and the jamb, a couple of inches below the lock, with just enough of it showing so that he could feel it with a fingertip. Then he locked the door, put himself and the pack inside the Jeep, and joined the rush of platelets heading for the heart of the Vegas creature.

TWO

THE HOT LICKS CLUB wasn't just a jazz spot. Like just about every other entertainment spot in Vegas, it was dominated by a ground-floor casino and it had a theme—a broad mix of 1920s speakeasy and 1930s supper club. Wall murals and furnishings reflecting that bygone era, jazz music blaring over loudspeakers, employees decked out in period costumes that ranged from tuxedos and gowns to gangster-style and flapper outfits. Combined with the neon glitz-and-glitter of the casino, the effect was ludicrous. But the customers didn't seem to think so. The casino was packed, the slots and tables getting heavy play, streams and knots of gawkers clogging the narrow aisleways.

Fallon found his way to an escalator at the far end. Propped up there was a large billboard sign that read: BENNY AMATO AND HIS JAZZBOS. VOCALS BY HELEN DUPREE. APPEARING NIGHTLY EXCEPT SUNDAY IN THE INTIME ROOM. DIXIELAND, SWING, FUSION. DINNER AND DANCING TILL THE WEE HOURS. There was a photo of a group of eight men and one woman, all wearing the requisite period clothing. The man in the foreground holding a trumpet was black and middle-aged, but neither he nor any of the other Jazzbos was identified by name.

On the second floor, a velvet-roped aisleway led to a wide set of closed doors. A neon sign above them bore the standard '30s tilted cocktail glass and the words INTIME ROOM in blue letters. Another billboard in front of the doors announced that the Intime Room opened for dinner at 7:00 and that the music started at 9:00. Nearby was a gated ticket window staffed by a smiling young woman painted up like a Busby Berkeley hoofer. Fallon put on a smile as he walked up.

Before he could say anything, the woman said in a chirpy voice, "We're sold out for supper, sir, but bar space is still available. The Intime Room has *three* bars," she added, as if she were awed by the fact.

"Can I ask you a question before I decide to buy a ticket?"

"Oh, sure. About the Jazzbos?"

"Yes. I thought I recognized the trumpet player in the billboard photo downstairs. Eddie Sparrow?"

"Yes, sir. That's right."

"Well, I knew Eddie in San Diego," Fallon lied. "Is there any chance I could see him for a couple of minutes, say hello?"

"You mean now? Oh, I don't think he's here yet. The musicians don't usually come in until about an hour before they're ready to go on."

"They allowed to mingle on their breaks between sets?"

"With the customers? Oh, sure. The management likes them to do that."

"You said three bars. They have names?"

"Names? No, they're just bars. You know, one on each side and one in back where you go in."

"So I can pick any one I want."

"Oh, sure. Wherever there's room. But you have to buy a ticket."

Fallon said patiently, "I will. I'd also like to leave a message for Eddie."

"Message? You mean with me? I won't see him when he comes in—I'll still be working here in the booth."

"You could pass it on to someone who will see him, couldn't you?"

"Pass it on?" she said doubtfully. "Well . . . I guess I could."

On a page in his notebook Fallon wrote: *I'm a friend of Court Spicer. I'll make it worth your while if you'll give me a couple of minutes during your first or second break. Look for me at the bar nearest the entrance, white man, blue shirt, tan suede jacket.* He signed it *Rick*, folded the paper twice, and put it and three bills into the tray under the window gate.

"The extra ten is for you," he said.

Her smile got even brighter. "Thanks! I'll pass it on. The message, I mean."

"One more question," he said as he pocketed the ticket. "Would you know of a casino where the employees wear gold sleeve garters with black ruffles?"

"Sleeve garters?"

"Like women's garters, only around their upper arms."

"Oh." The smile turned into a thinking frown. "Gold with black ruffles . . . well, I know I've seen them somewhere . . . Oh! Oh, sure, the Golden Horseshoe."

"The Golden Horseshoe."

"It's in Glitter Gulch," she said. "You know, the Fremont Street Experience?"

Glitter Gulch. The Fremont Street Experience. That was downtown Vegas, a mile or so north of the Strip—five blocks of casinos, restaurants, lounges in a covered mall dominated by a ninety-foot-high, multimillion-dollar Viva Vision screen, the largest on the planet. One of the city's big attractions. Fallon had gone there once with Geena—for ten minutes, all he could stand of a constant assault on the visual and aural senses. Larger-than-life animations, integrated live video feeds, synchronized music on a high-tech canopy the length of more than five football fields. State of the art fiber-optic light shows and what was billed as 550,000 watts of concert-quality sound.

Deafening noise, to him. The kind that shattered silence like a sledgehammer powdering glass.

Two minutes inside the mall and his head ached; his eyes felt as raw as if he'd been staring into the noonday desert sun. Milling, jostling crowds as thick as those on the Strip. Shills offering come-on gambling packages, hawkers handing out prostitutes' calling cards and extolling their services even though prostitution was technically illegal in the City Where Anything Goes. Walking here or on the Strip on a Saturday night was like being trapped on the shrieking, neon midway of a madman's carnival.

It was almost a relief to walk into the Golden Horseshoe. Almost. Electronic bells and whistles and bongs and burbles, rattling dice and clicking chips and clinking glassware, chattering human voices, laughter, shouts and cries and all the other myriad sounds made by men and women caught up in the gaming fever—a pulsing din that kept rising and being bounced

back down from the low glass ceiling. Didn't matter what casino you entered during peak times, from the megaglitz palaces to the low-roller clubs
like this one—the noise level was the same. Loud, loud, loud.

The motif here was Western, the old Hollywood movie variety. Waitresses dressed like saloon girls, croupiers and dealers and stickmen and pit
bosses in ruffled shirts and string ties and cowboy boots. And all of them
wearing gold armbands with black-ruffled edges.

Fallon took a long, slow walk around the casino. Making it look casual
when he paused near one of the blackjack, craps, or roulette layouts for a look
at a male employee who more or less fit Casey's description of Banning.
None of them had a dragon tattoo or wore a cat's-eye ring.

A crowd of people was grouped around one of the crap tables, hooting
and hollering whenever the dice were rolled. Fallon stepped over that way for
a look at the stickman, all but invisible in the crush, whose droning voice reminded him of the handful of crap games he'd gotten into in the army.

"Ee-o-leven, a winner! Pay the line. Same lucky shooter coming out . . .
Eight, hard way eight, eight a number. Place your come and field bets
Nine, eight the point . . ."

Once more the dice rattled off the board. This time the crowd groaned.

"Ace-deuce, three craps—a loser. Pay the field . . . New shooter coming
out. Place your bets . . . Seven! Seven, the winner. Pay the front line . . ."

Fallon moved on.

After a second circuit, to make sure he hadn't missed anybody, he went
into a raised, neon-lit lounge bar. The Western-etched leather stools were
mostly filled, the barman busy, but only half the tables were occupied, mostly
by players studying the big keno board on one wall. He picked a table along
the outer rail, at a distance from the nearest players. A tired-looking cocktail
waitress, thirtyish, wearing a Miss Kitty outfit and one of the distinctive
sleeve garters, drifted over. He ordered a beer. When she brought it, he laid a
ten-dollar bill on her tray.

"Busy night," he said.

"I've seen it a lot busier."

"Bet you have. Been working here long?"

She gave him an up-from-under-look.

"Don't worry," he said, "I'm not going to hit on you. I asked because I'm looking for a guy I know. I've been told he works here."

"Is that right?"

Fallon said, "No, keep it," as she started to hand over his change. "If you've been working here a while, you probably know him. This friend of mine."

"Maybe. What's his name?"

"Well, he called himself Banning when I knew him."

"Called himself? What does that mean?"

"Claimed he had a good reason for not using his real name." Fallon shrugged. "Don't ask, don't tell."

"I don't know anybody named Banning," she said.

"So maybe now he's using his real name again. He's in his midthirties, heavyset, kinky black hair. Dragon tattoo on his right wrist, wears a gold cat's-eye ring on his left hand."

She made a face. "Doesn't sound like a guy I'd want to know. What do you want with him?"

"He owes me some money."

"Yeah, I'll bet. What are you, anyway, some kind of cop?"

"Do cops give out five-dollar tips?"

"I don't know any cops," she said. "Or any Bannings. Or any guys with dragon tattoos. Thanks for the tip." And she walked away.

Wrong approach. But what was the right one, given the sketchy information he had?

Fallon took one more stroll around the casino floor. This time there was activity on a raised stage set back into a long alcove at the rear. Tinny piano music blared and spotlights shone hard and bright on eight young women in skimpy costumes dancing a Western movie version of the can-can. Each wore one of the gold-and-black garters, not on their arms but on their bare thighs.

Ah, Christ, he thought. Dancers, cocktail waitresses, blackjack dealers—all the women employees wore them. And there didn't seem to be any difference between a Golden Horseshoe sleeve garter and leg garter. The one Casey had seen at the motel didn't have to've been Banning's. It could just as easily belong to a girlfriend who worked here.

Some detective, Fallon. Jumping to conclusions, missing the obvious.

Maybe he was out of his league in this kind of hunt; maybe he wasn't the right man for the job after all. It might be smarter to turn the legwork over to a professional. Sam Ulbrich, or someone like him. Foot the bill, and then stand off with Casey and wait for results.

No, the hell with that. Geena's knock on him: not aggressive enough, not a fighter anymore—a quitter. Besides, detectives were expensive and he didn't have unlimited funds, and there were no guarantees a pro would be able to find out any more than he could. Ulbrich hadn't found Spicer and the boy, had he?

All right. Man up and use his head from now on.

He rode the escalator to the second floor, where there were a steak restaurant—Old Billy's Texas Grill—and a coffee shop. He sat in one of the coffee-shop booths, tried a new approach on the woman who waited on him.

"I'm looking for a friend of mine. He might work here, might be a friend of one of the woman employees—I'm not sure which." And then Banning's description. Casual, offhand. No mention of the name Banning.

Craps—a loser.

After eight by the time he finished picking at a bad tuna salad. He tried the same line on the cashier while he paid his check, and when he went back down to the casino, on a different cocktail waitress.

Craps again.

THREE

THE INTIME ROOM RESEMBLED an oversized 1930s nightclub laid out in a circular fashion, with the three bars and the stage forming an outer ring around an inner one of close-packed tables lit by blue lamps and a par-queted dance floor. Waiters in tuxedos circulated among the tables; even the bartenders were in soup-and-fish. New Orleans-style jazz music blasted from loudspeakers. Benny Amato and his Jazzbos were onstage, warming up for their opening set with riffs and trills and runs that you could hear when one of the recorded pieces ended. The place was packed, standing room only at the bars. Fallon's choice of the rear bar had been the right one. It was the least jammed of the three because it was the farthest from the performers.

He jostled his way to a position at one end. The stage was a long way off, but he had a clear enough look at the musicians. Mixed group—Latino, African-American, Caucasian. The piano man appeared to be the leader, Benny Amato. The rest were drums, bass, alto sax, tenor sax, trombone, cornet, and Eddie Sparrow on trumpet. Sparrow sat slumped on a stool, do-ing less noodling with his instrument than the others. He was even smaller in the flesh than he'd appeared in the group photo, maybe five and a half feet tall and a hundred and twenty pounds. He didn't look as if he could blow a dozen riffs without losing his wind and keeling over.

Fallon knew a little about jazz. Geena's brother Stephen was a nut on it, had insisted on dragging them to jazz clubs and festivals in the L.A. area. He liked it well enough, in small doses—the bluesy, sweet-and-lowdown pieces more than the wailing, frantic arrangements. There wouldn't be much of the former here tonight, he figured, but he was wrong. The Jazzbos mixed it up pretty well, up-tempo and down-tempo, classics and less well-known compositions and a few that were probably of their own devising.

The first set was strictly Dixieland, which meant that they'd do swing, probably thirties-style New York or Kansas City, for the second set, and fusion—jazz elements mixed with pop, rock, folk, R&B—for the third. Their late-hour sets would be a mix of all three, with plenty of improv for the true aficionados who would rather linger here than head downstairs to the gaming tables.

They had the usual repertoire of standards: "When the Saints Go Marching In," "Saint James Infirmary," "Basin Street Blues," "Stompin' at the Savoy," "Take the A Train," "Blues in the Night," "Perdido," "Gloomy Sunday." Mixed in were vocals featuring the dark and slinky Helen Dupree: "Moanin' Low," "Jazz Me Blues," "Skeleton Jangle." Good group, all right, with Amato's piano and Sparrow's trumpet dominating the instrumentals. Despite his slightness, Sparrow seemed to have more energy and stamina than any of the others. Plenty of talent, too. His solos earned him enthusiastic applause.

When the first set ended, Fallon watched the musicians file off. Some of them went backstage, while three others, Eddie Sparrow among them, moved out through the audience. It took Sparrow six or seven minutes of handshakes and brief conversations to make his way to the rear bar. When he got close, Fallon stepped out and went to meet him.

"Eddie. Eddie Sparrow."

The little man focused on him, ran liquidy brown eyes over him. "You Rick?" he asked in a surprisingly husky voice.

Noise and people swirled around them. Fallon had to stand close and lean down to hear and be heard. "That's me. You blow a mean trumpet, Mr. Sparrow."

"Thirty years of lip, man. Jazz your business, too?"

"Not like it's yours. Buy you a drink?"

"Never use it. Come on, we'll talk out front. Too crowded in here."

Fallon followed him out and a short distance away from the entrance. When Sparrow stopped, he said, "Five minutes, that's all I got for you."

"Five's plenty."

"So why the note? What's worth my while?"

"Court Spicer. I'm trying to find him."

"You're not the only one."

"I heard the two of you were friends, so I thought maybe—"

"Friends, hell," Sparrow said. "That dude don't have any friends. You're not one any more than I am. What you want with him?"

"Personal business."

"Money business?"

"Among other things. I'll pay cash for his current address."

Sparrow laughed, showing three or four gold teeth. "If I knew it, you could have it for free."

"So you don't know if he's living in Vegas now?"

"Not a clue."

"Or if he is, where he might be playing?"

Shrug. "Bound to be a joint, solo or with some crappy trio. Spicer's strictly second-rate."

"You ever play a gig with him here?"

"Never. Once, in San Diego, when I needed some quick cash. Once was enough."

"He played Vegas about three years ago. You wouldn't have been here then, by any chance?"

"Three years ago? Uh-uh. I was with the Jazzbos in L.A."

"Something went down around that time, something that brought Spicer some heavy cash. Any idea what it was?"

"You mean a gambling score?"

"Any kind of score."

"Not that I heard about. That cat's mojo is strictly bad."

Fallon let it go. "I understand you saw him not too long ago."

"Yeah, I saw him. Jam over in Henderson last Sunday."

"Talk to him?"

"No, man. He was leaving when I got there," Sparrow said. "Did a fast fade when he saw me."

"Like he was trying to avoid you?"

Shrug. "We never did have much to say to each other. And him and the dude he was with seemed to be in a hurry."

"What dude? You know him?"

"Never saw him before."

"What'd he look like?"

"Mean-looking, that's all I remember."

"Dragon tattoo on his right wrist?"

"Tattoo . . . yeah. Dragon breathing fire."

Banning.

"You said this gig was in Henderson. Where, exactly?"

"Some rich cat's hacienda in the desert. He's a buff. Throws regular jazz parties, pays high and handsome for the best improv talent. Must've been a hundred people at this one."

"What's his name?"

"Rossi. Big wheel in one of the chemical outfits over there."

"You remember the address?"

"No. Benny made the arrangements."

"Maybe you could ask him? It's worth a hundred to me."

"Forget it, man. He knew I was out here talking to you, he wouldn't like it. Besides, you don't need an address. That hacienda's all by itself on a hill, mesa, whatever they call 'em out here. Biggest place around, you can see it a mile off when it's lit up at night."

"What part of the desert?"

"East. Far enough out you can see the lake from up there."

"Lake Mead?"

Sparrow shrugged, then glanced at the gold watch on his wrist. "Five minutes are up."

"Pay you something for your time?"

"Oh, five skins'll do it."

". . . Five hundred dollars?"

"You said worth my while, right?" Sparrow laughed again, gave Fallon a broad wink. "Jerking your chain, man. You planning on giving Spicer a hard time when you find him?"

"Yes. A hard time."

"Then you don't owe me a thing."

*   *   *

Late-night quiet at the Rest-a-While. Neon sign, office lights, scattered nightlights; everything else was shadows. Fallon shut off the Jeep's lights as he rolled past the office; pale desert moonlight guided him into a space two doors down from number twenty. He lifted the pack off the floor where he'd stowed it, swung it onto his shoulder as he stepped out. He walked soft to the room door, paused to listen, then slid his hand down along the jamb below the lock.

The piece of toilet paper was gone.

He keyed the door open and shoved it inward, standing back to one side. Nothing happened. A thin trail of moonlight penetrated the darkness within, showing him a portion of the carpet and one corner of the rumpled bed. He stayed where he was for a minute, listening to unbroken stillness. Finally he moved forward, reached around the jamb, found the light switch and flicked it on.

Empty. Come and gone, whoever the intruder was. Went away frustrated, likely, because Fallon hadn't left anything of himself in the room.

He dumped the pack on the bed and went right back out again, locking the door behind him. The office lights were on, but so was the night latch. A different clerk, in his sixties and gray-bearded, sat reading a paperback behind the desk. Fallon rang the night bell. The clerk stood up like a soldier coming to attention. He took his time walking over, peering warily at Fallon through the glass.

"Help you, sir?"

"I'm one of your guests." Fallon waggled his room key to prove it. "Talk to you for a minute?"

The clerk relaxed, shrugged, went back behind the counter and buzzed him in. "Problem with your room?"

Fallon said, "No. Just wondering what time the day clerk comes on. Charley, isn't it?"

"No, his name's Max."

"Now where did I get Charley from? Max, you said? Max what?"

Brief hesitation before the clerk said, "Arbogast. You have some sort of problem with him?"

"Not that type, is he? Hard to get along with?"

"Everybody's hard to get along with sometimes," the night man said.

His expression and the pitch of his voice indicated that he didn't much like Max Arbogast.

"Complaints about him from other guests?"

"You want to make one, Mr.—?"

"Spicer. Court Spicer." The clerk didn't react to the name. "No," Fallon said, "I just need to talk to him about a friend of his, comes to the Rest-a-While sometimes—midthirties, heavyset, tattoo on the back of his right wrist, wears a cat's-eye ring. You know him?"

Again, no reaction. "Doesn't ring any bells."

"Max wouldn't happen to live here, would he?"

"Would you live here if you didn't have to?"

"When'll he be in in the morning?"

"He won't. Tomorrow's Sunday. One of his days off."

"Maybe I can catch him at home then. You know where he lives?"

"Couldn't tell you if I did. Rules."

"Sure. Rules."

There was one Arbogast listed in the phone directory. M. Arbogast, 1189 Ocotillo Street, North Las Vegas. The right one? He'd find out in the morning.

The room had a cramped, airless feel and he slept restlessly. He was awake for a good hour before dawn, up and dressed and on his way just as the pink-and-gold sunrise colors began to seep through the sky.

FOUR

OCOTILLO STREET: SEVERAL BLOCKS of lower middle-class, low-rise apartment buildings stretched out between two thoroughfares. Number 1189 was two stories of one- and two-bedroom units, built of stucco and wood and arranged in a squared-off horseshoe with the closed end facing the street. A sign above the entrance read: DESERT VIEW APARTMENTS. Sure. Right. If you took a ladder and a pair of binoculars up onto the roof, maybe. From the apartments, all you'd be able to see were urban glimpses that might have been of any city in the country.

It was a few minutes past seven, Sunday morning quiet, when Fallon found a place to park on the crowded block. He locked the Jeep with all his belongings inside, walked to where a cactus-bordered path led to the building's entrance—a set of glass doors that were closed but not locked. When he passed through, he was in a tunnel-like foyer that opened into a central courtyard. He scanned the row of mailboxes until he came to the one marked 2-D. The name tag on it, Max Arbogast, removed all doubts about the phone book listing.

From the courtyard Fallon could see that the apartment entrances opened onto wide concrete walkways, motel fashion. Except for a central section of palm trees and low-maintenance ground cover around the pool area, the Desert View resembled the Rest-a-While. Man in a rut, Arbogast. Or maybe this type of structured environment was his comfort zone.

Apartment 2-D was in the near wing, second floor, with access by elevator or outside staircase. Fallon climbed the stairs, walking soft. Each unit was set off from its neighbor by short stucco walls that created a narrow little sitting area and gave the illusion of privacy. A curtain was drawn across the window alongside the door marked 2-D. Through the glass he could hear the hum of an air conditioner, even though the early morning was cool. The television was on in there, too, indicating that Arbogast was awake.

He put his thumb on the bell button and left it there until he heard footsteps approaching. There was a short silence—Arbogast looking through the peephole in the door—and then a muttered "Oh, Jesus!"

"Open up, Max."

Arbogast said more clearly, "What's the idea, what do you want?"

"Talk. Open the door."

"No. Go away."

"Talk to me or talk to the police."

". . . The police? Listen, you can't—"

"Want me to say it louder, so your neighbors can hear? I can make a lot of noise before I call the cops."

Nothing for a few seconds, while Arbogast wrestled with a decision. Then a chain rattled, the lock clicked, the door opened a few inches. Fallon pushed it inward, saw Arbogast backing away into the center of a cluttered room, went in and shut the door behind him. The apartment smelled of coffee, stale food, unwashed clothes. Your typical sparsely furnished bachelor's quarters: dirty dishes, empty beer bottles, newspapers and clothing strewn over the floor, the TV set blaring away in one corner. The television was the only new, clean-looking item in the room—a 42-inch flat-screen job.

Arbogast was in his bathrobe, a coffee cup clutched in both hands against his chest as if he were afraid Fallon might try to take it away from him. Grayish beard stubble flecked his thin cheeks; what hair he had left was puffed out in little tufts around his head like a collection of dust mice.

"What's the idea coming here this time of day, threatening me with the cops?"

"Turn off the TV."

". . . What?"

"The TV. It's too damn loud. Turn it off."

Arbogast stared at him a few seconds longer, finally went to where a remote control unit lay on an end table and used it to stop the noise. Then he sidestepped to a breakfast bar that separated the living area from a kitch-enette, set the coffee cup down and leaned back against it.

"That's better," Fallon said. He moved forward until only a couple of feet separated them. "Now we can talk."

"I don't have anything to say to you. What you want? How'd you find out where I live?"

"Banning."

"Who? Listen, I told you—"

"I know what you told me. Now you can tell me the truth."

"I don't have to tell you anything. I don't know anything."

"Like I said. Me or the police."

"You can't sic the cops on me, I haven't committed any crime—"

"No? How about an illegal search, for starters?"

"A . . . what?"

"Illegal search. You searched my room last night after I left the motel."

"I never did. That's a damn lie—"

"Then there's accessory to rape and aggravated assault."

"What?" Arbogast's hand spasmed; coffee slopped from the cup onto the sleeve of his robe.

"That's what Banning was doing in room twenty last Wednesday. Rap-ing and beating up Casey Dunbar. And you helped him do it."

"No! I never did!"

"He told you she was coming in. He told you to give her room twenty and make sure the rooms near it were empty. He told you to destroy the registration card afterward."

Arbogast shook his head. He looked as though he wanted to crawl down inside his robe and hide there, like a turtle retreating into its shell.

"I didn't know," he said in a cracked voice. "I didn't know."

"What didn't you know?"

"A favor, that's all. He gave me a hundred bucks. You think I can't use a hundred bucks?"

"What'd he tell you was going on?"

"He wanted to talk to her, that's all. Private, he said. Just talk to her. I swear to God—"

"But he didn't just talk to her and you know it. Bloodstains on the bed, the bathroom towels. Right? The maid found them, or you did."

"Maria. I had to give her some of the hundred so she wouldn't . . . Ah, Jesus, listen, you got to believe me, I didn't know . . ."

"When I checked in yesterday," Fallon said, "you called Banning and told him I was there and asking questions. Then you called him again after you searched my room."

"I had to. He said . . . I didn't know why you were there, who you were, I still don't know, I *had* to call him."

"What's his real name?"

"No, I can't tell you that . . ."

Fallon stepped closer, caught a handful of the soiled robe in a hard fist. Arbogast made a squawking noise, flinching and cringing.

"What's his name, Max?"

"I . . . oh shit, all right, all right. Bobby J."

"J-a-y?"

"No, the initial. J."

"Last name?"

"I don't know his last name."

"Come on, Max."

"I swear I don't know, I swear!"

Fallon let go of the robe. Arbogast moved away from him, running his hands over the fabric—drying them. Cool in there, almost cold from the air conditioner, but he was sweating visibly now.

"Where does Bobby J. live?"

"I don't know that either."

"You've got his phone number, but you don't know his last name or where he lives. You expect me to believe that?"

"It's the truth, I swear to God."

"How do you know him, then?"

"He . . . listen, you're not gonna tell anybody about this, are you? It could, you know, it could do me some hurt."

"How do you know him?"

Arbogast said, looking at Fallon's ear the way he had at the Rest-a-While,

"He brings women to the motel sometimes. For parties. And he don't want anybody to bother him when he's there."

"What women?"

"You know. Hookers."

"Don't bullshit me, Max," Fallon said. "Prostitution may be illegal in Vegas, but it still runs wide open. He doesn't need to bring hookers to a place like the Rest-a-While, or you to watch out for him if he did."

"Women, that's all. Women he picks up . . ."

"Underage girls. That's it, isn't it? Runaways, jail bait."

Arbogast made a sound in his throat.

"What is he, some kind of pimp?"

"No. I don't know. He just likes to party with young girls . . ."

"Party. Drugs as well as sex, right?"

"I don't know nothing about drugs."

That was a flat-out lie. He knew, all right. He swiped his hands across the robe again.

"So this Bobby J. paid you to keep other guests away from the rooms he was using and warn him if anybody complained or the cops showed up."

"Listen, you have to understand . . . my salary isn't much, and my rent . . . A man has to live, don't he?"

"How does Bobby J. live, if he's not a pimp?"

"I don't know."

"Drugs? Dealer as well as a user?"

"I tell you, I don't know. I don't *want* to know."

"What's his connection with the Golden Horseshoe?"

"Huh? Oh . . . Candy."

"Who's Candy?"

"His woman. He brought her with him a couple of times."

"She work at the casino?"

"Dancer. They got this French can-can show . . ."

"What's her last name?"

"I don't know. Just Candy."

"Describe her."

"Blonde. Tall, legs up to here, nice tits."

Fallon said, "Court Spicer."

"Huh?"

"Name mean anything to you?"

". . . Your name, isn't it? That's how you signed the register."

"What'd Bobby J. say when you told him Court Spicer was asking about him?"

"Wanted to know what you looked like. What kind of car you drive, from what state."

"What did he say then?"

"Just . . . look in your room, see what I could find out from your stuff."

"And when you called him again and told him there wasn't any stuff?"

"Keep an eye on you, let him know if you tried to pump me again."

"All right. What's his phone number?"

". . . You're not gonna call him up? You do, he'll know where you got it . . ."

"Not if I tell him otherwise. You're not the only person in Vegas with his number."

Arbogast gave it to him, reluctantly. "Just don't tell him you been talking to me, okay, Mr. Spicer?"

Fallon said, "My name's not Spicer," and left Arbogast standing there sweating in his cold apartment.

FIVE

Sunday morning slow at the Golden Horseshoe. Red-and-gold curtains were drawn across the stage where the can-can dancers performed. More than half the roulette, craps, and blackjack tables were covered; at a couple of the others and among the banks of slots, a scattering of players, pale and zombie-eyed, sat trying to recoup their losses. A cleaning crew ran a phalanx of whirring vacuum cleaners over the worn carpets.

Fallon sat down at an open but empty blackjack table and tried working the bored woman dealer for information on Candy. It cost him twenty dollars on four lost hands, the last two when he had paired face cards and the dealer hit twenty-one, plus a five-buck tip to find out that the stage show started at one o'clock on Sundays. If the dealer knew Candy, she wasn't admitting it.

He tried the bartender in the lounge, one of the cocktail waitresses, another waitress in the coffee shop. The only one who could or would tell him anything about Candy was the cocktail waitress, but for another five dollars it wasn't much.

"I know her, sure," she said, "but I don't think she works Sundays."

"Where can I get in touch with her?"

"I wouldn't tell you that even if I knew. Besides, she's not available."

"I'm not planning to hit on her. That's not why I want to talk to her."

"Yeah, sure. Well, whatever you want with Candy, you don't want anything to do with her boyfriend."

"Is that right? Why not?"

"Trust me, you just don't."

Fallon asked the boyfriend's name. The waitress gave him a cynical, humorless smile, shook her head, and walked away.

"Another favor? Getting to be a habit." But Will Rodriguez didn't sound annoyed. He had a wife who talked nonstop, three rambunctious kids, and an even temperament; it took a lot more than an early Sunday morning call to raise his blood pressure. "What is it this time?"

"I've got a phone number and I need the name and address that goes with it. Think you might be able to get me a match today?"

"I suppose I can try, if it's important."

"It is."

"Uh-huh. Anything else you want?"

"Background on whoever the number belongs to, if you can manage it."

"Hey, why not. I had nothing better to do today than spend time with my family."

"I wouldn't ask if there was any other way, Will."

"I know, I know. Let me get a pen . . . Okay, what's the number?"

Fallon read it off to him.

"Seven-oh-two area code. Las Vegas."

"That's where I am now."

". . . Vegas can be a rough town, amigo."

"I can take care of myself."

"The Dunbar woman there with you?"

"Not yet. Still resting in Death Valley."

"But you'll be hooking up with her later."

"Not the way you mean."

"You think her ex-husband and son are there, is that it?"

"I don't know yet," Fallon said. "That's why I need the name and address."

Will made a noise that could have been a laugh or a snort. "I never knew they had windmills in the Nevada desert."

"What's that mean?"

"Think about it," Will said. "I'll get back to you."

Windmills. Christ.

Fallon drove back to the Rest-a-While. He'd put another piece of toilet paper under the door lock when he left; it was still there. No need to go inside—all his belongings were stowed in the Jeep. He walked through the gathering heat to the motel office.

Yet another clerk was behind the desk, this one a wheezily fat woman with dyed yellow hair. Any messages for room 20? No messages. He asked her if she knew a man named Bobby J., added the man's description. No again. It didn't sound like a lie; her expression remained bored and disinterested.

There wasn't much point in staying here any longer. Bobby J. had to be curious who he was, why he'd come to the Rest-a-While using Court Spicer's name, but evidently not curious enough to initiate contact. Either that, or the decision to play a waiting game had been Spicer's. As far as one or both knew, Fallon didn't have any idea who Bobby J. was or how to find out. The beating and rape hadn't been reported; they were in the clear as long as they did nothing to call attention to themselves.

He wheeled the Jeep over to the freeway, took Interstate 15 south to McCarran International. There were a lot of motels in the vicinity; he picked a Best Western with a VACANCY sign on Tropicana Avenue, checked himself in under his own name. As before, he brought his pack into the room, left everything else locked in the Jeep.

Late morning by then. He used his cell phone to call Vernon Young's home number in San Diego. This time he got a person, a woman, instead of the answering machine. He asked for Vernon Young and she went and got him.

"You don't know me," he said when Young came on the line, "and my name isn't important. I'm a friend of Casey Dunbar."

Longish silence. Then, "How is she? Is she all right?"

"Yes."

"Is she with you? Let me talk to her."

"She's not here right now."

"Where's 'here'? Where are you calling from?"

"Las Vegas."

"Did she ask you to get in touch with me?"

"No, it was my idea. About the money she owes you."

"What money?"

"The two thousand dollars she borrowed."

". . . She told you about that? What else did she tell you?"

"Enough about what happened to her son to put me on her side."

"The boy? Spicer? Did she—?"

"No, not yet."

". . . You're helping her?"

"Yes."

"Another detective?" Young sounded flustered.

"Not exactly."

"Then just who are you?"

"I told you, a friend."

"Is there some reason you won't give me your name?"

There wasn't. "It's Fallon."

"She never mentioned anyone named Fallon. How long have you known her?"

The intense, proddy type, Vernon Young. But then, under the circumstances he had a right to demand answers. "It's a long story, Mr. Young. She can tell you how we met if she wants to. About the money—"

"I'm not concerned about the money, I'm concerned about Casey."

"She'd be grateful if you'd give her time to pay you back."

"Yes, yes, as much time as she needs. I should have given her the money in the first place."

"Maybe let her keep her job, too?"

"Yes, of course," Young said. Then, "Spicer and the boy . . . are they why you're in Las Vegas?"

"It's possible they're here. We just don't know yet."

Pause. "No offense, Mr. Fallon, but you're just a voice on the phone. I'll feel better about all this if I can talk to Casey. You understand?"

"I understand."

"I would appreciate it if you'd ask her to call me as soon as possible. Will you do that?"

Fallon said he would.

Casey answered her cell so fast, she must have been sitting with it in her hand. "I thought you'd never call," she said. Spirit, eagerness in her voice today.

"I've been busy."

"Have you found out anything yet?"

"A few things. Nothing definite. How're you feeling?"

"I'm all right. But if I have to stay in this cabin much longer, I'll start climbing the walls."

"Your car fixed?"

"Yes. And yes, I'm up to the drive down there. Where are you?"

Fallon told her the name and location of the Best Western. "I'll make a reservation for you when we hang up," he said. "If I'm not in my room when you get here, wait in yours until I get back."

"Where will you be?"

"I don't know yet."

"For God's sake, don't be evasive."

"I'm not. I *don't* know yet where I'll be. You just have to let me do things my own way. I won't withhold anything important from you."

". . . All right."

"One piece of news: I just spoke to Vernon Young."

"What? You called him? For God's sake, why?"

"To get the money situation straightened out. It's okay, he's on your side. You can take as much time as you need to pay back the two thousand. And you can keep your job."

"He . . . said that?"

"Yes. He sounded pretty worried about you."

"You didn't tell him what I tried to do to myself?"

"No."

"What did you tell him?"

"That I'm a friend helping you try to get your son back. Not much else.

He wants you to call him to confirm it and that you're okay. I think it's a good idea. He seems to care about you."

She didn't say anything. Faint muffled sounds came over the line. Crying a little? If so, she didn't want him to know it. He made it easier for her by saying he'd see her soon and then breaking the connection.

Different from any woman he'd ever known, Casey Dunbar. A bundle of conflicted, deep-seated emotions. He had a feeling that her depression and her self-destructive impulses were caused by more than the situation with Spicer and her missing son. Self-doubts, more than a little self-hatred. Other things, too, that he couldn't fathom—like trying to see through dark, turbulent water.

Better not try too hard to understand her and her private demons. He had enough of his own to deal with.

SIX

HENDERSON WAS A DESERT community seven miles southeast of Vegas, off the highway that led to Boulder Dam. The fastest-growing city in Nevada, according to advertising billboards, as if that was an attraction to be recommended. Gateway to the Lake Mead National Recreation Area.

Fallon took the downtown exit and passed several big chemical plants, following signs that said HISTORIC WATER STREET DISTRICT. Once he got there, the whole character of the town changed. Luxury resorts and the usual casinos, art galleries, boutiques—much of the architecture art deco–themed. Henderson was no longer just an industrial center, where half of the state's nontourist industry output was produced. It had changed its image, gone upscale. Home base now for the wealthy and the upwardly mobile who liked their surroundings and their recreations less gaudy than those in Vegas proper.

He found a parking garage off Water Street, went back and joined the flow of walkers and gawkers. All of the shops were open; no dark Sundays in places like this. He found a gift shop that sold local maps, bought one, and carried it into the lobby of a nearby casino hotel. There were several roads that snaked out into the desert to the east, he found. To cover them all, blind, would take too long.

Once he left the hotel, it took him less than five minutes to locate a real estate agency. The woman he spoke to was eager to please when he said he was in the industrial chemical business, in the process of moving to the area from California, and in the market for a new home.

"We have several excellent listings, Mr. Spicer. How large a home are you interested in?"

"At least four bedrooms. With some open space around it. Would you have anything in the vicinity of the Rossi home?"

"Rossi?"

"Works in the same industry I do. Big home on a mesa."

"Oh, of course. David Rossi, from Chemco."

"That's right."

"Well, you know, that's quite an exclusive section . . ."

"Not a problem."

That widened her smile. "Well, then, let's see what we have on or near Wildhorse Road."

Wildhorse Road ran due east through miles of new housing developments, finished and under construction, unchecked growth that would eventually swallow up every available mile of desert landscape west of the Lake Mead National Recreation Area. Beyond its present outer limits, where open desert still dominated, a few larger and more expensive homes appeared at widely spaced intervals. In the distance, then, he could see the low mesa rising up off the desert floor, the hacienda that stretched like a huge sand-colored growth across its flat top.

A little over a mile and he was at the base of the mesa, where a paved lane led up to stone pillars and a pair of black-iron gates. Stone walls extended out on both sides to make sure you didn't drive onto the property unless you were invited. An electronic communicator was mounted on a pole just below the gates. Fallon stopped alongside, rolled his window down, reached out to punch the button that opened the line.

Pretty soon the box made noises and a Spanish-accented woman's voice said, "Yes, please?"

"Is Mr. Rossi home? David Rossi?"

"What is your name, sir?"

Fallon didn't hesitate. His own name wouldn't get him in; only one name might. "Spicer. Court Spicer. It's important that I talk to Mr. Rossi."

"Wait, please."

He switched off the ignition. With the window lowered and the Jeep's engine shut down, the desert afternoon should have been quiet, but it wasn't. Even out here he could hear the engines, literally. A small plane sliced through the air overhead, making a rumbling whine. When it passed, the accelerating roar of a couple of racing dune buggies rose out of the distance. That was the thing about the desert-eaters: they were never silent.

Ten minutes passed. He was thinking that he'd been blown off without a callback when a loud electronic buzzing sounded and the gates began to swing inward. He drove through, climbed the asphalt drive between low stone walls. When it leveled off at the top, he was in a sandy parking area large enough to accommodate fifty or more vehicles. Some view from up here, as long as you faced toward the east—sage-dotted desert and distant shimmering water.

Up close, the house seemed almost fortresslike. It was built of native stone with a tile roof that gleamed redly in the sun glare. Seven or eight thousand square feet, Fallon judged, maybe more. Yucca trees and desert plantings, and a flagstone walkway, separated it from the parking area.

A middle-aged Latina opened the door to his ring. She didn't say anything, just stepped aside so he could walk in. Dim and twenty degrees cooler inside. The woman led him down a hallway, through a massive sunken living room: tile floors, muraled walls, dark-wood furnishings, Indian rugs and pottery. Casual elegance. Geena would have loved it.

The entire inner wall was floor-to-ceiling windows and sliding glass doors. Through the glass, Fallon could see that the hacienda had been built around a central courtyard as large as a parade ground: more yuccas and plantings, stone benches, a swimming pool surrounded by flagstones and outdoor furniture. Sitting at one of the umbrella-shaded tables was a woman in a floppy brimmed sun hat—the only person in the courtyard.

The woman got to her feet as the maid led Fallon outside, stood waiting as they approached. There was a glacial look about her despite the hot sun: thin white robe that covered a slender body from throat to ankles, the sun hat white with white-gold hair showing beneath the brim, white skin. Her expression was cold, too, but it changed slightly, her eyes narrowing and her mouth opening an inch or so, when she got a clear look at Fallon.

"All right, Lupe. That will be all." She continued to look at him, unblinkingly, as the maid drifted away. The gray eyes were as cold the rest of her. She might have been a mature thirty-five or a face-lifted forty-five.

When they were alone, she said, "I'm Sharon Rossi," without offering her hand.

"It's your husband I wanted to see, Mrs. Rossi."

"My husband left this morning on a business trip. Perhaps I can help you, Mr.—Spicer, is it? Court Spicer?"

"No. My name is Fallon."

Her unpainted mouth shaped itself into a faint, humorless smile. "You told Lupe you were Court Spicer. A ploy to get yourself admitted?"

"Yes."

"Why? What do you want with my husband?"

"To ask him about Spicer."

"Why?"

"I think he may know the man, know where I can find him."

"Why do you want to find him?"

"Personal reasons."

"I see. Do you have identification, Mr. Fallon?"

He opened his wallet, slid out both his driver's license and his Unidyne ID. She studied them for a full minute each, as if memorizing the data they contained, before she handed them back.

"Sit down," she said then. "It's cooler under the umbrella." She waited until he was seated before sitting again herself. On the table next to a cloth pool bag was a pitcher of pale-green liquid with ice cubes and lime wedges floating in it. "Would you like a margarita?" indicating the pitcher. "They're very good. Lupe's special recipe."

"Nothing, thanks."

Sharon Rossi poured her glass three-quarters full, took a sip that lowered it to the halfway mark. Her movements were slow, deliberate, and for the first time, watching her, Fallon realized she was a little drunk.

"Now then," she said, "I'd like to know exactly why you want to find Court Spicer."

"First tell me this. Is Spicer a friend of your husband's?"

"I highly doubt it."

"Business acquaintance?"

"No."

"Friend of yours?"

"Hardly.

"Then why did you agree to see me?"

"Your motives first, Mr. Fallon. Then we'll get to mine."

Lay it out for her? He couldn't see any reason not to, up to a point. He said, "When I find him, I'll also find his son."

"His son." The way she said the words told him she hadn't known about the boy. "And why do you want to find his son?"

"Spicer kidnapped him four months ago, in San Diego. No one's been able to find them since. The boy is eight and a half, asthmatic, and his mother is desperate to get him back."

"I see. And what is your interest?"

"Let's just say I'm a friend of the mother."

"Your Unidyne card says you're a security officer. Does that mean you have experience in detective work?"

"Not if you mean finding people. Military police for four years, private security work for the past dozen."

"I see," she said again. Another sip of her margarita. She seemed to be thawing a bit. Maybe it was the liquor, maybe what he'd told her. Or maybe a little of both. "What made you come here to ask about Court Spicer?"

"A jazz musician who knows Spicer saw him at a jam here last Sunday."

"Ah, yes. David's all-consuming passion for jazz."

"Did you see Spicer then?"

"I saw him, yes."

"Talk to him?"

"No. We have nothing to say to each other."

"So he's been here before. At other parties."

"But not to listen to the music. On business, I think."

"What kind of business?"

"My husband prefers not to tell me that."

Fallon said, "Spicer was with a man called Bobby J. last Sunday."

"Was he? I wouldn't know."

"The initial J. Bobby J." Fallon described him. "Familiar?"

"Vaguely. I seem to recall the tattoo. But there were quite a lot of people here. There always are at one of my husband's jams."

"His jams?"

"Ours," she amended, but a faint resentment lingered in her voice. David Rossi was the jazz buff, not his wife.

"Was Spicer playing at the Sunday jam?"

"No. He wasn't a spectator either. He and my husband spent some time together in David's study."

"Any idea why?"

"No, but I'd like to know. I'd very much like to know." Sharon Rossi drank again before she added, "My motives now, Mr. Fallon."

He waited.

"Do you know anything about my husband?"

"Not much, no."

"He's usually very sure of himself. I've never known him to be afraid of anything or anyone—except Court Spicer."

"How do you mean, afraid?"

"Just that. Nervous, on edge—afraid. Every time Spicer has come here, David has looked and acted the same, during and afterward." She made a low, mirthless chuckling sound. "It's almost Pavlovian, the effect that man has on him. And I haven't a clue why. The one time I asked him about Spicer, he told me to mind my own damn business."

Fallon asked, "How long has he known Spicer?"

"I'm not sure. A while."

"More than three years?"

"At least that long."

"How often does Spicer show up here?"

"Not often. And when he does, judging from David's reaction, it's without an invitation."

"I wonder if your husband knows where he's living now."

"He might. It would depend on their business, wouldn't you say?"

"What do you think that business is?"

She poured her glass full again, drank deeply this time. The thaw was complete now; there was high color in her cheeks, a faint glaze on her eyes.

She was the type of drinker who knew her limits and seldom exceeded them, but she seemed to feel she had cause today. Dutch courage for what she was about to reveal.

"I think Court Spicer has some sort of hold on my husband," she said. "I think he comes here for money, large amounts of money."

"Blackmail?"

"Or extortion. I probably shouldn't be telling you this, but David keeps a large sum of cash in his safe. The morning after the last jam, I opened the safe and there was quite a bit less than there should have been."

"How much less?"

"Five thousand dollars."

Spicer's outside source of income—not much doubt of that now. He must have stumbled onto something three years ago, something David Rossi didn't want revealed, and been using it to bleed him ever since.

Fallon asked, "So you thought I was Spicer coming back for more. What were you planning to do?"

"Confront him."

"Just like that?"

"No." She reached into the pool bag, came out with nickel-plate and pearl shining in her hand. "With leverage."

It wasn't much of a gun. A .32-caliber automatic slightly larger than her palm. Lethal enough at close range, but unreliable at any distance.

"Suppose he wasn't intimidated," Fallon said. "What would you have done then?"

"Would I have shot him? I don't know, I might have."

"It takes a lot of courage to shoot a man."

"Or a lot of provocation. When it comes to protecting my nest, I'm as much of an animal as any wild thing."

Fallon believed it. He said, "Why tell me all this, Mrs. Rossi? It's personal and you don't know me, you didn't even know I existed until a few minutes ago."

"Isn't it obvious? You have a good reason for finding Court Spicer and you seem determined to do so. When you do, you'll be in a position to find out what hold he has on my husband. And to recover anything in his possession that might be . . . shall we say embarrassing?"

Fallon said nothing.

"The idea doesn't appeal to you? You're big and strong, Spicer is small and soft. You shouldn't have any difficulty."

Still didn't say anything.

"If you agree," she said, "I'll pay you the same amount my husband gave Spicer—five thousand dollars. And if you succeed, I'll double that amount."

He said carefully, "I'm not in this for money. Money isn't important to me."

"Oh, come on now. Money is important to everyone."

"Not me."

"So noble. Just doing a favor for a friend. Why not do what I ask and make it two favors, the second one paid for?"

It sounded good on the surface. Return a kidnapped boy to his mother and at the same time put an end to a blackmail or extortion game. Recoup his expenses and make a profit, whether he succeeded or not. But there were pitfalls. As things stood now, all he had to do if and when he located Spicer was to call the police and have him arrested on the kidnapping charge. What Sharon Rossi wanted meant confronting the man, maybe threatening him, maybe leaning on him. Breaking the law. Another thing: suppose the hold Spicer had on David Rossi involved a felony of some kind? Suppose there was incriminating material and he could lay hands on it? If he turned it over to Sharon Rossi or her husband for pay, he'd be guilty of withholding evidence, compounding a felony. He could go to jail.

"Well, Mr. Fallon?"

"I don't think so," he said. "No."

"Why not, for God's sake?"

He told her why not.

"False concerns," she said. "Whatever Spicer's hold, it can't possibly involve a serious crime. I know my husband—he's not capable of a criminal act. Infidelity, oh yes, and questionable business practices, yes indeed, but those are his limits."

That was the liquor talking. Nobody knows anybody else as well as they think they do, and that went double for wives and husbands.

"I'm sorry. The answer is still no."

"There's nothing I can say to convince you?"

"No."

It was several seconds before she said, "Suppose I could help you find Court Spicer."

"How could you do that?"

"I have access to my husband's personal records. It's possible he has Spicer's current address written down somewhere or stored on his computer."

"If that's the case, why haven't you looked before? Or have you?"

"Yes, but mainly I was searching for something that would explain Spicer's hold on David. I may have overlooked an address or phone number. Or failed to look in the right place. *Would* you do what I ask in exchange for that information?"

Fallon thought about it. Worth yet another gamble?

He was still thinking when she said, "I could confront Spicer myself, of course. But then I'm not particularly brave or aggressive outside the confines of this house. And it might compromise your efforts to return the child to his mother."

"Yes, it might."

"I could hire someone else to do the job. A professional. That might work to both our benefits."

"It might also trade one blackmailer for another. There aren't many reputable detectives who'd take on a job like this."

"I'd run the same risk with you, wouldn't I?"

"I'm not that kind of man."

"No, I don't think you are," she said. "I wouldn't have been as candid with you if I did. Which leaves you as my only option. Will you please help me?"

It was the "please" that made up his mind; the way it came out told him it was not a word she used often. "All right, Mrs. Rossi," he said. "If you can give me a lead to Spicer, I'll try to find out what you want to know."

"And any . . . material you might recover?"

"You'll get it, as long as it doesn't put me in a legal bind."

"I'll have to be satisfied with that, then, won't I," she said.

Fallon traded his cell phone number and the name and location of the Best Western for her private number. "How long will it take you to search?" he asked then.

"Not long, unless I have to go to David's office at Chemco. If there's anything to find, I'll have it tomorrow at the latest."

She stood up when he did, steady on her feet despite all she'd had to drink. He didn't think she'd keep on boozing after he left. Woman with a purpose now. The drinking was a product of loneliness and a less-than-happy marriage, but it was plain that she loved her husband and would do whatever was necessary to keep the relationship intact.

In a way, Fallon thought, she was a lot like him. A fighter at heart. All either of them really needed was something worth fighting for.

SEVEN

WILL RODRIGUEZ GOT BACK to him just as he was leaving the Henderson city limits. "I had to call in a favor of my own to get what you asked for," Will said. "You owe me big time, amigo."

"I know it. I won't add to the debt."

"Number you gave me is a cell phone registered to a woman named Harper, Constance Harper."

Constance Harper. Constance—Candy's real name? In character for a man like Bobby J. to use a phone registered in his girlfriend's name.

"What's the address?"

"Twenty-nine hundred Cactus Flower Court, unit twenty-two-B, Vegas."

"Anything on her? Known associates, anything like that?"

"Not without a lot more checking than I had time to do. Pretty common name. What does she have to do with the missing kid?"

"Directly, nothing," Fallon said. "But if I catch a break, she could be a way to find him."

Twenty-nine hundred Cactus Flower Court turned out to be a collection of forty or so town-house-style apartment buildings, four units to each, that took up an entire block a mile northeast of the Strip. Long entrance drive at one end, rows of covered carports for the tenants, an open visitors' parking area nearby. Low-maintenance desert landscaping with crisscrossing crushed-rock paths.

Fallon put the Jeep into one of the visitors' slots and went first to check the carports. Each one was marked with a unit number; 22-B contained a dark blue Lexus a couple of years old—not the kind of car you'd expect a strong-arm pimp or a dancer in a Glitter Gulch casino to be driving.

He followed one of the paths into the complex. Kids and adults made a lot of Sunday-afternoon noise over at a pool and picnic area. The town houses were arranged in geometrical rows, separated by plantings and paths; he found his way to the building numbered 22. Apartment B was ground floor, its front windows and one beside the door covered by blinds.

When the door opened to his ring, it was on a chain and half of a woman's face appeared in the aperture. A wrinkled, sixty-something face topped by gray-streaked red hair. The one eye studied him warily.

"Yes?"

"Constance Harper?"

"That's right. I don't know you. What do you want?"

"Is Candy here? Or Bobby J.?"

"Who?"

"Candy, from the Golden Horseshoe. Her boyfriend, Bobby J."

"Never heard of them. You got the wrong unit, mister."

"He has a dragon tattoo on his right wrist—"

That was as far as he got. She shut the door in his face.

Fallon went back to the Jeep with his teeth clenched tight. The woman hadn't lied to him. The liar was Max Arbogast.

The son of a bitch had deliberately given him a wrong phone number.

Arbogast wasn't home. Or if he was, he wasn't answering his door.

Mild hunger prodded Fallon into a shopping-center coffee shop a few blocks from the Desert View Apartments. Lousy food and two glasses of weak iced tea used up half an hour. One more pass at Arbogast's apartment, he decided, before he went back to the Best Western.

He couldn't have timed it better. As he came down Ocotillo Street, Max Arbogast was just getting out of a parked Hyundai with a grocery bag under one arm.

Fallon swung the Jeep into a space opposite. Arbogast was on his way up the path to the entrance by then; he didn't see Fallon cross the street and come up fast behind him, didn't know he was there until he said, "Hey, Max."

Arbogast stiffened, turning. "You again."

"Me again. You don't seem surprised to see me."

"What you want now?"

"The truth this time."

"Truth? What're you talking about?"

"Let's go up to your apartment."

Arbogast gnawed on his lower lip, little nibbling bites like a rat gnawing on a piece of cheese. "No. I had enough of that this morning."

"Your car, then. Just so we have a little privacy."

"I got nothing more to say—"

Fallon closed fingers around scrawny biceps, squeezed hard enough to make Arbogast wince. "Your car. Now."

They went to the Hyundai. Arbogast unlocked the passenger door and Fallon prodded him inside, then slid in behind him. With the door shut, the car smelled of dust and leftover fast food. The grocery bag contained a six-pack of beer; Arbogast ran his hands over it, looking at Fallon's ear again.

"You gave me the wrong phone number for Bobby J."

"The hell I did."

"The hell you didn't. Let's have the right one."

Arbogast hesitated, but only for a few seconds. The number he recited then was close to the one that belonged to Constance Harper, but not that close.

"If that isn't right," Fallon said, "I'll be seeing you again. And you won't like what happens."

"It's right. I swear it."

"Like you swore it this morning. What else did you lie to me about?"

"Nothing, for Chrissake."

"So you told me everything you know."

"Everything, yeah."

"I don't think so. I think you know or have some idea where Bobby J. lives or works or hangs out."

"No."

"Listen, Max. I'm going to find him one way or another, and when I do I'll either drop your name or I won't. Be straight with me and I never heard of you. Keep lying, and I'll make him believe you sold him out for cash."

Arbogast did some more lip-gnawing. The thin hands kept on moving restlessly over the bag.

"Okay. Okay. Cheyenne Street."

"What about Cheyenne Street?"

"He's got a place there. In back."

"In back of what?"

"Slot machine repair business."

"His?"

"I don't know. His, some friend's, I don't know. I had to take him something there once. A package."

"Drugs?"

"A package."

Fallon sat looking at him for a time. All he saw was pale profile; Arbogast still wasn't making eye contact.

"What's the street number?"

"Nine eighty."

"That better be right, too."

"It is, it is. Nine eighty Cheyenne."

Arbogast opened the driver's door, quick, as if he were afraid Fallon might try to stop him. He didn't even wait for Fallon to get out so he could lock the car again, he just started running for the Desert View's entrance.

The Jeep's GPS pinpointed the Cheyenne Street address. Northeast Las Vegas, not too many miles from the Desert View Apartments. But Fallon didn't go that way; he went south to the Best Western instead.

Casey was at the motel, her Toyota slotted in front of the unit he'd reserved for her. He parked next to it, rapped on the door.

"How long have you been here?" he asked when she let him in.

"About two hours." She caught hold of his arm, gripped it tightly. "What've you found out? Anything?"

"A few things. Getting closer."

"To Court and Kevin? They're still in Vegas?"

"That I don't know yet."

"Well, for God's sake, what *do* you know? You promised you wouldn't hold out on me, Rick."

"I'm not trying to."

He filled her in. As much of what he'd discovered as he thought she should know at this point. She paced while she listened. Tense and restless after the long drive and long wait, but she seemed all right otherwise. She'd made an effort with her appearance, either for him or for herself: hair combed, lipstick on her scabbed lips, makeup covering the healing marks on her face. The tight-fitting blouse and skirt she wore made him aware that her figure was well-developed.

"What now?" she said when he finished talking. "Just wait for the Rossi woman to call? Suppose she doesn't, then what?"

"Don't get ahead of yourself. I'm going out again."

"Where? To do what?"

"To see what I can find out about Bobby J."

"Let me go with you."

"No. It's better if I do this alone."

"I did enough sitting around at Furnace Creek. I'll go crazy if I have to keep doing the same thing here."

"It won't be for long. Go over to the coffee shop next door, have a drink or two at the bar."

She started to argue, changed her mind and sat down heavily on the bed. Fallon said, "I'll need the keys to your car."

"My car? What for? What's the matter with your Jeep?"

"Nothing's the matter with it. How much gas is in the Toyota?"

"I don't know, I had it filled before I left. Rick . . ."

"The keys," he said. "I'll try not to be too long."

EIGHT

A BLACK-PAINTED SIGN ON the cinder-block building at 980 Cheyenne Street said: CASINO SLOT MACHINE REPAIR AND RESTORATION. MECHANICAL AND ELECTRONIC SLOTS. ANTIQUE BALLY'S, MILLS, JENNINGS—SALES AND REPAIR. The building, in a semi-industrial area off I-15, looked to be thirty or forty years old and in need of a paint job. On one side was a parking area that extended around to a narrow loading area at the rear; another cinder-block edged over close on the far side. Two entrances were visible from the street, the main one in front and a side door off the parking area. The only car on the property, a bulky, dusty Ford Explorer, was parked twenty yards or so from the side door.

Fallon took all of this in on a slow drive-by. The place looked closed up, deserted despite the Explorer. The sun, big and hazy orange, had drifted low in the western sky; where its descent was blocked by buildings and trees, shadows gathered in pools and pockets along the cinder-block's wall.

He circled the block. There was no rear access to Casino Slot Machine Repair from the next street over; you could see the lines of its roof, but that was all. When he turned back onto Cheyenne, he made sure there was nobody in sight and then parked the Toyota a short distance away, underneath a droopy palm tree on the opposite side of the street. Good vantage point: both front and side entrances and all of the parking area.

He picked up the 7×50 Zeiss binoculars from the seat beside him, slid down to a level where he could rest the glasses on the sill, and adjusted the focus until everything over there came into sharp relief. Next to the side door was a window with blinds drawn behind it. The powerful glasses showed him bars of light between the slats.

Nothing out of the ordinary. Nothing to arouse suspicion. Just the Explorer, the otherwise empty lot, the side door, the lighted window.

Setup.

Trap.

He'd figured it that way from the first; that was why he'd switched cars. Arbogast's lack of surprise, his shifty-eyed nervousness, the too-quick way he'd given up the Cheyenne address—all red flags. The little bastard must have contacted Bobby J. after Fallon's first visit, told him about giving out the wrong phone number, been told in return what to say and do if Fallon came back to brace him again. Fallon was asking too many questions for Bobby J. to keep ignoring him. So the trap had been set to find out who he was and why he was snooping around, and then to get rid of him one way or another—threats, a beating, maybe even a permanent disappearance. The desert surrounding Vegas had a reputation as a missing-persons graveyard.

Well, none of that was going to happen. Not here, not tonight.

Fallon waited, the Zeiss glasses on his lap. There wasn't much activity in a neighborhood like this on a Sunday evening—an occasional car or truck passing by, but no pedestrians. The steady traffic hum on I-15 was audible but muted.

Sunset, dusk settling. And the cinder-block's side door opened and a man eased out into the lot.

Fallon snapped up the binoculars. The man was built like a pro football lineman, with a mane of yellow hair and a yellow beard—not Bobby J. He walked out past the Explorer, to gaze up and down the street in an agitated way. Looking for a black Jeep, so he didn't pay any attention to the parked Toyota Camry. After a few seconds he returned to the side door, paused to light a cigarette, then went back inside.

So there were at least two of them. And it didn't look as though they were as good at waiting as Fallon was.

Full dark came quickly, as it always does in desert country. Lights blossomed in the front windows of the cinder-block—Judas lures, for all the good it would do them. The rest of the property remained dark. The only other lights in the vicinity were on street poles, none close to the Toyota.

Another hour went by. The side door opened again and the yellow-bearded man came out and repeated what he'd done before, the fast, hard way he moved and a slapping gesture of one hand against his pant leg suggesting both frustration and anger. He stayed out there less than a minute. Fallon watched him go back inside, heard the faint slam of the door.

How much longer would they wait?

Not too long. Less than forty-five minutes.

The front window lights went out first. A couple of minutes later, the side door opened, blackness replaced the light inside, and two figures emerged. Fallon put the glasses on them; the Zeiss's capacity for clear night vision was the best on any pair of commercial binoculars he'd used. The one who locked the door matched Bobby J.'s description. His face was tight-set and he seemed to be arguing with the bearded man as they crossed to the parked Explorer. Not Bobby J.'s vehicle, evidently; he got in on the passenger side.

Fallon drifted lower on the seat, his eyes on a level with the sill, as the Explorer's headlights came on and the machine swung around fast, burning rubber. It was headed his way as it came off the property; the beams splashed over the Toyota. He sat up, reached for the ignition as soon as it shot past.

The Explorer was at the intersection when he completed his dark U-turn. As soon as it turned left, toward the freeway, he put the headlights on and increased his speed. Once he made the turn, he was less than a block behind.

He maintained that distance onto I-15 south, then slipped over into a different lane and dropped farther back. The Explorer, with its high rear end and fat taillights, was easy to keep in sight. The way Yellow Beard was driving, moderate speed, no lane changes, said that they didn't know he was there. Even if they'd considered the possibility of a tail, it would be his Jeep they'd be alert for.

Vegas proper was where they went. The Charleston Boulevard exit, then half a mile west along there and into a deserted but well-lit shopping center. Fallon rolled on past, watching in the rearview mirror as the Explorer braked alongside a low-slung, light-colored car parked near the entrance. Bobby J.'s wheels. Yellow Beard dropping him off.

Fallon caught a green light at the next intersection, turned right, and pulled to the curb. From there he watched the Explorer U-turn, head out of the lot the way it had come in, and make a cross-traffic left turn back toward the freeway. Bobby J. had closed himself inside the light-colored car; its headlights flashed on. If he drove away in the same direction as Yellow Beard, keeping him in sight and catching up wouldn't be easy.

But he didn't. Piece of luck there: the light-colored car came shooting across the lot, at an angle to where Fallon waited, exited and turned right onto the same four-lane cross street. Mustang, one of the original models, white or beige. Fallon gave its taillights a full block lead before he swung out to follow.

And that was when his cell phone rang.

He almost didn't answer it. Tailing another car at night was tricky enough without any distractions. But the noise grated on him, and Bobby J. was still moving in a straight line and about to be held up by a red light at the next intersection. Fallon yanked the phone out of his pocket, flipped it open.

"Mr. Fallon? This is Sharon Rossi."

"Yes, Mrs. Rossi."

"I think I may have found what we're looking for. I'm not sure, but I don't see what else it can signify."

The light was green now and they were rolling again. A rattletrap pickup had cut in between the Toyota and Bobby J.'s Mustang. Fallon swerved into the other lane. Sharon Rossi's voice droned in his ear, telling him what she'd found was a piece of paper under the blotter on her husband's desk, in a handwriting different from his.

"Go ahead, what's on the paper?"

"The name on it is Steven Courtney. That could be the name Spicer's using, don't you think? The same initials—"

"What else?"

" 'Care of Co-River Management, Laughlin.' "

"Laughlin."

Bobby J. was about to make a left-hand turn. No signal, just the flash of brake lights and a rolling stop as he waited for a break in the oncoming traffic. Fallon couldn't get over behind him in time; the pickup, forced to slow, too, was blocking the lane.

"That's all," Sharon Rossi said. "No address or phone number."

Fallon passed the Mustang just as Bobby J. completed the turn, then cut into the inside lane. There was a left-turn lane at the intersection ahead, the light green. He hit the gas hard.

"Mr. Fallon?"

A quick glance into the rearview mirror showed him the Mustang just disappearing into a side street up ahead. He snapped, "Emergency, I'll call you back," and threw the phone onto the passenger seat so he could grip the wheel with both hands.

The light flashed yellow as he veered into the left-turn lane. He kept on going, out into the intersection in a sliding U-turn. Got the Toyota straightened out, accelerated to the side street and made the turn just in time. Near the end of the next block ahead, taillights threw a sheen of crimson on the darkness and the Mustang made a sharp left and disappeared behind a low wall.

Residential street: older tract houses on small lots. Fallon reduced his speed to twenty-five. The wall, he saw as he neared, was whitewashed stucco—a boundary between two of the houses. The one beyond had a huge tangle of prickly pear cactus growing in the front yard. The Mustang was in the driveway, dark now and drawn well back toward the rear. As Fallon passed, its door opened and a dome light came on and the dark shape of Bobby J. emerged.

Fallon drove on to the next intersection. A street sign there said he was on the 200 block of Sandstone Way. He turned right onto Pyrite Way, circled that block onto the first cross street—Mineral Way—and came back onto Sandstone. Short of the corner, he parked and shut off the lights. And sat there to let his pulse rate slow while he did some thinking.

What he felt like doing was going to the house on Sandstone, taking Bobby J. by surprise, and beating the crap out of him—payback for what he'd done to Casey, and what he and Yellow Beard had planned to do at Casino Slot Machine Repair. Stupid idea, fueled by ragged emotions. It could get him arrested for trespassing and assault, for one thing. Or the tables turned and the crap beaten out of *him*: he wasn't armed and he didn't know who else was in that house.

Besides, Bobby J. wasn't the important issue here. Finding Court Spicer, reuniting Kevin and his mother, was. He hated the idea of letting a man like that get away without paying; but he wasn't a crusader, he wasn't even a law officer—it was not up to him to dispense justice. Sooner or later Bobby J. would take a fall, a hard fall. His kind almost always did.

Fallon started the car and headed back to the Best Western to tell Casey the news about Laughlin.

PART III
LAUGHLIN

ONE

THEY LEFT FOR LAUGHLIN early Monday morning. Fallon would have preferred to make the drive alone, but Casey wasn't having any of that. Not that he blamed her. If her son was somewhere in the Laughlin area, she needed to be there when he was found. Compromise: she'd agreed to stay in the background, let him handle things in his own way. She followed him to McCarran International and left the Toyota in long-term parking, and they went together in the Jeep.

Laughlin was ninety-five miles south of Vegas, on the Nevada side of the Colorado River boundary with Arizona. The state's newest gambling hot spot, with a string of big hotel and casino resorts along the riverfront. Another desert-consuming creature spreading out on both the Laughlin side and across the river in Bullhead City, where most of the casino service people lived. Fifty thousand population in the area now and more coming in all the time, for the gambling and the related jobs, the fishing and boating on the Colorado and Lake Mohave, the lure of desert-country retirement living. And every day, more open space disappeared and the creature spread closer to Spirit Mountain on the east, the gold-and-silver-bearing hills beyond Bullhead City—wilderness areas that Fallon had explored when he was stationed at Fort Huachuca, and again on a packing trip with Geena not long after they were married.

Casey had wanted to leave right away last night, as soon as he told her Sharon Rossi's news, but he'd talked her out of it. There was no good reason to make the long drive until daylight; their only lead was Co-River

Management, and whatever kind of business it was, it was bound to be closed at night. Only the casinos ran twenty-four hours.

She'd been upbeat and animated then—a glimpse into the kind of woman she must have been once, before the deterioration of her marriage and the loss of her son and the rape and beating that had driven her to attempted suicide. Animated, trusting, likable. Attractive, too. She had a nice smile, a warmth that softened the hard edges created by adversity and depression.

This morning, though, she'd retreated inside herself again. She had little to say as they headed south on 95. She sat stiff and tight-drawn, hunched forward a little on the seat, eyes steady on the surface of the highway; the only time she spoke in the first thirty miles was to ask him to drive faster, even though he was pushing it as it was, at seventy-five.

He tried to start a neutral conversation, draw out some details about her life. All he could get were thumbnail sketches: Born and grew up in Chula Vista. Two years at San Diego State, majoring in business administration and "more drunken parties than I can remember." A couple of menial jobs before she answered an ad and Vernon Young gave her a chance to work first as a receptionist and then as a sales agent. Interests? Kevin. Reading—biographies, mostly. Romantic movies. Music, but not jazz, she'd had all she could stomach of her ex's brand of music. Future plans when she had the boy back? Keep him safe, make sure he grew up to be a better man than his father. She didn't answer when Fallon asked her what she wanted for herself.

After a time, he found himself shifting the conversation to his relationship with Timmy, the things they'd enjoyed doing together. She listened, but all she contributed were monosyllables. She didn't ask him about his background, and he didn't volunteer any information. He didn't like talking about the early part of his life.

But he couldn't keep the memories from intruding as he drove. The near-slum neighborhood in East L.A., his low-income civil servant father, his alcoholic waitress mother, the crime-ridden streets, the crappy schools, the daily struggle during his teenage years to avoid the lure of gangs and drugs. If he hadn't gotten out by joining the army when he turned eighteen, God knew what direction his life would have taken. He might have ended up in a dead-end job like Pop's, living poor and eventually dying in that miserable neighborhood the way his parents had, Pop of a heart attack at fifty-four while Fallon was at Fort Benning, Ma two years later of too much booze, too many long hours waiting tables, too much grinding poverty.

The army had given him hope, discipline, pride, a sense of honor and justice, the desire to build a better life for himself. And then Geena had given him the rest of what he needed. He'd met her in Tucson in the last year of his tour. Driven over from Huachuca with a couple of buddies, and there'd been a party, and there she was—pretty, sweet-natured, as lonely and as hungry for love as he was. They'd gotten married as soon as he was discharged. Moved back to the Encino area when the Unidync job offer came up, Geena already pregnant the first time. Difficult pregnancy; she'd miscarried in her fourth month. Three years later, after another difficult pregnancy, Timmy had been born. And the future looked as bright as his boyhood had been dark.

Until Timmy's accident. Until it all collapsed.

Now he was ready to rebuild another future, one that suited the man he'd evolved into after his son's death. The third stage of the life of Richard Fallon. Put on temporary hold by Casey Dunbar and his commitment to her, but that was all right. True peace of mind didn't come easy; sometimes it came only after you were put to a test. This was his test. This was the price he felt obligated to pay.

It was midmorning when they reached the junction with State 163, near the Arizona border, and turned there toward Laughlin. Hotter down here than it had been in Vegas; heat mirage pulsed liquidly off the asphalt ahead. The desert country in this corner was more sun-baked, even, than Death Valley. The hottest day anywhere in recorded U.S. history, Fallon remembered reading somewhere, had been in Bullhead City in 1983—132 degrees in the shade.

When they were traveling on 163, Casey stirred and asked, "How much farther is it?"

"Less than twenty miles."

She ran her hands along the front of her thin skirt, then extended them out toward the air-conditioning ducts. "I keep wondering," she said then.

"About what?"

"Kevin. If he's all right."

"Dry heat like this should be good for his asthma."

"Yes, but how is Court treating him? Is he allowed to go out, go to school? Is somebody watching him when Court's working? Or is he being locked up in some sweltering room somewhere?"

"Don't. You can make yourself crazy with that kind of worrying."

"I'm half crazy already," she said. "You ought to know that if anybody does."

Despite its rapid growth in recent years, Laughlin was still a small town. The population sign they passed on the outskirts read 8,629, which made it five times smaller than Bullhead City. Most of the growth seemed to be to the south and east in the direction of bare, raggedy Spirit Mountain— housing tracts, schools, malls. The main drag, Casino Drive, followed the line of the river and was crowded with tourist-related businesses on the east side, the big casino resorts all fronting the Colorado like a miniature version of the Vegas Strip—Don Laughlin's Riverside, named after the town's founder, Colorado Belle, Edgewater, River Palms, half a dozen others.

As early as it was, people streamed along the sidewalks and on the river walk that wound its way behind the casinos, and you could see pleasure boats trailing milky wakes on the sun-bright water. The Colorado, the West's most important water source, had a shrunken look—the result of the worst drought in a century, nine years long now and counting. Another couple of years and a shortage would probably be declared and the Department of the Interior would reduce water deliveries to Arizona and Nevada, if not southern California. Nature paying humanity back for its encroachment and its decades of waste.

One of the streets that angled off Casino Drive to the east was Bruce Woodbury Drive. That was where Co-River Management was located, in a new office park, in a building with three other small businesses. A sign on the front cleared up the minor mystery about its function; it was a property management outfit that handled residential and commercial rentals and leases and new home sales.

As he parked in the facing lot, Fallon debated letting Casey come inside with him. She might be able to get information more easily than he could because of her real estate license: professional reciprocity. But he decided against it. The marks on her face, the scabbing and chapping and peeling sunburn, hadn't healed enough to be fully concealed by makeup.

He said, "You'd better wait here." She didn't argue, so he added, "I can leave the engine running if you want to stay cool."

"No, I need to get out and walk. I've been sitting too long."

Fallon left her and went inside. Co-River's anteroom resembled a doctor's office: half a dozen uncomfortable-looking chairs, tables with magazines and brochures, an L-shaped counter with a couple of desks behind it, a short hallway and a pair of closed doors. The one difference was the wall decorations: a three-by-six-foot architect's drawing of a housing development called Sunrise Acres, and an aerial photograph of the same development under construction.

Behind the counter were two women, one a youngish redhead, the other middle-aged, both of them working on computers. The middle-aged one pasted on a professional smile as Fallon approached, stood up to ask what she could do for him.

"I'm looking for one of your clients," he told her. "A man named Courtney, Steven Courtney."

"Yes?"

"He's a professional musician. Plays piano."

"Yes?"

"I've heard he's good and I'd like to talk to him, hear him play, maybe offer him a better deal than he has here. I own a small lounge up in Vegas that's just been renovated and I need some new talent for the reopening."

"I see." Her smile had slipped some; the bright version was reserved for prospective clients. "Why have you come to us?"

"I don't know where Courtney is working or living in the area," Fallon said, "but I understand he receives his mail here. So I thought you might tell me how to get in touch with him."

The rest of the smile disappeared. "We don't give out personal information about our clients."

"Not even if it's to their benefit?"

She shook her head. "If you'd like to leave your name and number, I'll see that Mr. Courtney gets it."

"I would, but I'm pressed for time. I need to hire a piano man as soon as possible. Couldn't you make an exception in this case?"

"No, I'm sorry, I'm not authorized to do that."

"Who *is* authorized?"

"Our director, Mr. Sanchez. But he isn't here. He's gone to a meeting in Fort Mohave."

"When will he be back?"

"I don't know," she said, tight-lipped now. "Possibly late afternoon, possibly not until tomorrow morning."

"That might be too late for Courtney and me. Couldn't you at least tell me where he's working in Laughlin?"

"I'm sorry, no."

The young redhead had been listening to the conversation while she tapped away on her computer keyboard. She said, "Oh, Lord, Jeanette, that's not privileged information. Why don't you just tell him?"

"Mind your own business, Kristin."

That came out sharp, and the redhead bristled and glared. "Don't tell me what to do. You're not in charge here."

"Neither are you."

Fallon said to the redhead, "Mr. Courtney will thank you for it," to take advantage of the friction between them. "I really am interested in hiring him."

Jeanette said, "I've already told you—"

Kristin said, "He's working at the Wagonwheel Casino, in their Sunset Lounge. I just looked up his file."

The older woman swung around angrily. "Mr. Sanchez will hear about this. Don't think I won't tell him, because I will."

"Go ahead. I'm just helping out a client, that's all."

"Now you listen here . . ."

They weren't interested in Fallon any longer, and he wasn't interested in their workplace bickering. He made a quick exit into the morning heat.

"I knew Kevin was here," Casey said. She'd taken off her sunglasses and her eyes were bright. "I knew it!"

Fallon said, "Maybe."

"What do you mean, maybe?"

"Bobby J. knows I've been asking questions and he's probably alerted Spicer by now. Spicer doesn't know who I am, but he can put two and two together and it's bound to spook him. If he's spooked enough, he's liable to start running again."

"But not this soon. He must believe you're still in Las Vegas, that you don't know he's in Laughlin."

"Maybe," Fallon said again.

"Kevin's here. I *know* he is, I can feel it."

"In any case, it's time we let the law take over."

"The police? In a little town like this?"

"Bring in the FBI, then."

"No," she said. "No."

"Why not?"

"They'd take their time before they did anything, that's why. Agents would have to come down here from Las Vegas to interview us, then they'd check with the management company, the casino, God knows who else to make absolutely sure Steven Courtney and Court Spicer are the same person, and then they'd have to plan and coordinate before they acted. I almost went crazy when Kevin was kidnapped, waiting for somebody to do something. You're in the security business, you must know that's the way they work."

He did know it. The law was methodical; no agency was going to rush out and arrest a man who might or might not be Spicer, and if they found the boy, hand him over immediately to his mother.

"It could take days," Casey said. "And what if that gave Court enough time to disappear with Kevin again? I'm so afraid for him, Rick."

Fallon said nothing.

"There's another thing, too. The authorities don't know Court like I do. He's capable of holding Kevin hostage, hurting him or worse. I think I've convinced you how dangerous he is, but what if I couldn't convince them?"

"They're professionals. They won't put Kevin at risk. If Spicer's still here, they'd arrest him while he's at the Sunset Lounge, separated from the boy."

"We could do the same thing in reverse, and much more quickly—wait until Court's at the lounge, make sure Kevin's safe, and then contact the FBI. That makes sense, too, doesn't it?"

"In theory. It would depend on where Kevin is, whether he's alone or being guarded, how easily he could be rescued."

"It won't take long to find out, now that we know where Court's working." She gripped his wrist with fingers like talons. "I've waited so long, I can't wait much longer. I want my son back *now*."

"It's not going to happen immediately, no matter what we do."

"But soon. Soon. Just you, us, no police or FBI yet. Please?"

It went against his better judgment, but she was so eager, so desperate. There was no good argument against spending one day trying to locate the boy themselves, as long as they were careful. At the very least, they should be able to find out by tonight whether Spicer and Kevin were still in the Laughlin area.

There was another thing, too—Fallon's promise to Sharon Rossi. She'd brought them to this point; he owed her the effort to keep it.

"All right," he said. "We'll do it your way."

TWO

THE WAGONWHEEL HOTEL AND Casino was one of the smaller, newer resorts along Casino Drive. It didn't look like much in proximity to the Colorado Belle, one of the gaudier gambling palaces built to resemble an old Colorado River steamboat that bulked up next door. The covered-wagon design was spoiled by modern architectural modifications and too much splashy neon. The front entrance simulated a huge revolving wagon wheel, and you entered by following one stationary lighted spoke into the hub.

Fallon went in alone here, too, Casey waiting in the Jeep in a public parking lot nearby. There wasn't much chance Spicer would be at the Wagonwheel this early, but why run the risk?

The casino was moderately crowded, the banks of electronic slots getting most of the play, and the usual pulsing clamor made Fallon clench his teeth. The Sunset Lounge was on the second floor. A pair of marquee posters behind glass framed the entrance; he stopped to look at one of them. Medium-distance photo of a half-smiling man seated at a piano. Light-brown hair in a brush cut, light-brown goatee and mustache—not a match of Casey's description of Court Spicer. But the facial and body types were right, and it didn't take much imagination to picture him clean-shaven, with dark hair in a ponytail. The clincher, just discernible in the photo, was the mole on his left cheek near his mouth. Spicer, no mistake.

The lettering on the poster was all in black. Downcurving above the photo: STEVEN COURTNEY. Upcurving below it: KING OF THE IVORIES. Across the bottom: MOOD MUSIC FOR YOUR LISTENING AND DANCING PLEASURE. Trite and old-fashioned, aimed at the Baby Boomer generation. Fallon wondered if the poster was Spicer's doing, or a product of the Wagonwheel's PR staff.

The Sunset was the kind of lounge intended as an oasis for those who preferred quieter, more traditional surroundings. Stitched-leather booths, tables with leather chairs, a long neon-lit bar, a piano on a raised dais—seat empty, keyboard covered—and a small dance floor. Three big flashy keno boards served as reminders that this was first and foremost a casino lounge, with gambling the primary lure. Tinted glass composed the entire back wall so that you had sweeping views of the river, parts of Bullhead City and the Arizona desert stretching beyond.

There were only a handful of patrons at this hour, most of those grouped in one of the booths drinking Bloody Marys and marking keno tickets. The bartender, gray-haired, sixtyish, wearing a Western-style shirt and a string tie, stood slicing lemon and lime wedges with bored attention. Fallon sat down in front of him, ordered a glass of club soda with lime.

While the bartender poured it, Fallon said casually, "I noticed the posters on the way in. Steven Courtney, King of the Ivories."

"Yes, sir, that's right."

"I hear he's pretty good."

"Well, I wouldn't know about that. I work days."

"What time does he come on?"

"Six o'clock."

"Tonight—Monday?"

"Every night except Sunday, six till midnight."

"You wouldn't happen to know where I can find him now, would you? Where he lives?"

The bartender looked straight at Fallon for the first time. "No, I wouldn't," he said as he set the drink down. "Why?"

"He's an old friend. Happens I have some business with him."

"I couldn't tell you where the man lives even if I knew."

"Who could?"

Shrug. "Day shift manager, maybe, but he's not here. Why not just come back tonight?"

"I need to talk to Courtney as soon as possible."

"Well, you could check with the business office downstairs."

"Thanks," Fallon said. "I'll do that."

He did, and it was what he figured it would be, a waste of time. They wouldn't give out any personal information about their employees.

Casey said, "It's not even noon yet. What're we going to do for six hours?"

"The wait'll be longer than that. Fourteen or fifteen hours, at least."

"Why? Why so long?"

"I can't just walk in and brace Spicer at six o'clock, in front of a crowd of people. I'll have to wait until he's done playing for the night and follow him to where he's living. Just the two of us then. And, with luck, the boy."

"Oh, God. Isn't there any way to do it sooner?"

"I suppose I could talk to employees at the Wagonwheel and the other casinos, try to find somebody who knows him and is willing to give out his address. But the chances are slim, and there's the risk of word getting back to him."

"Yes, you're right. It's just that I can't stand waiting when we're this close to finding Kevin."

"You'll get through it."

"How? What are we going to do all day?"

"The first thing is find a place to have lunch—"

"I'm not hungry. I couldn't eat."

"—and then I'll get us a couple of motel rooms. After that, a long drive in the desert. Time passes more quickly when you're on the move."

"Another motel room? Why?"

"Place for you to be while I'm at the Sunset Lounge," Fallon said. "Place for you to spend the night—with Kevin, if I can make it happen."

"You will. You have to."

"We'll see. One step at a time."

* * *

They ate in a coffee shop on a side street off Casino Drive. Casey picked at
her food. Fallon ate most of his, slowly, not because he was hungry but to
kill an extra few minutes. Afterward, he found an inexpensive motel near the
Laughlin/Bullhead International Airport on the Nevada side of the river.
Separate rooms again, adjacent. He used up another half hour showering,
shaving, changing into a clean shirt. Casey hadn't bothered; she still wore
the same skirt and blouse, and her hair and face were still sweat-damp when
he knocked on her door.

He drove them over into Arizona, through Bullhead City and out past
Davis Dam and Lake Mohave, into the badlands toward the stark hills surrounding the old gold-mining town of Oatman. Fallon wondered if the re-
newable energy boom that had begun in the southern California deserts in
recent years would extend out here one day—geothermal power plants that
ran on hot water pumped from deep underground. Probably. Someday there
might well be vast solar energy farms in all of the western deserts, supplying
enough electricity for millions of homes and businesses. He had no objection to open space being used in this way, in the better-late-than-never battle to overcome the effects of global warming; the geothermal plants were
designed to be eco-friendly, to take up the least possible amount of space in
remote areas. Man finally taking positive steps to confine the crawling creatures, control the greed and waste that helped to feed them.

Casey showed no interest in the scenery or in the ghost buildings and
mining works that dated back to the area's first gold strike more than a century ago. She sat stiff and silent the whole way, and when he stopped in
Oatman and suggested that they have a beer, she let him lead her inside a
tavern like an animal on an invisible leash. She had the same tightly wound
inner focus on the way back.

It was nearly five when they reached the motel. She stirred then to look
at the clock on the dashboard. "Is that clock right? Five o'clock?"

"It's right."

"God, the time just crawls. I feel like I'm living in a vacuum. I don't
know how I'm going to get through another eight or nine hours."

He said nothing. There was nothing to say.

"What time are you going over there? To the casino?"

"Before six. I'll be there when Spicer starts playing."

"You're not going to talk to him?"

"Of course not. Don't worry, he's not going to know me from any other customer. I just want to get a look at him, watch him for a while. Then I'll come back here and we'll have dinner—"

She made a face. "No more food. I feel like puking right now."

"Dinner, and then we'll wait together until it's time for me to shadow him."

"I want to go with you."

"No. I thought we settled that."

"If he leads you to Kevin—"

"Then I'll call you first thing. It won't do either of us any good if you're there when I brace Spicer. You have to let me handle this my way, Casey."

"Your way. Your way." But she didn't argue anymore.

He said, "We'll play cards."

"What?"

"Cards. Gin rummy. You know the game?"

"Yes, I know the damn game."

"It'll help keep your mind off the clock."

"All right, gin rummy. Anything to make the time go faster. I'll even let you fuck me if you want."

The last words shocked him a little. Until he realized that that was all they were, just words. Meaningless, driven out of her by the yearning for her son and an abstract need for tension release and a calming of her inner turmoil. If he tried to take advantage of them, something he'd never do, she would either fight him off or submit like a rag doll.

He'd been sorry for her all along. Now what he felt was a kind of tender pity.

THREE

A T SIX O'CLOCK, THE Sunset Lounge was moderately crowded with cocktail-hour and predinner drinkers and sunset watchers. The fading sunlight that streamed in through the tinted windows had a mellow golden tone. Fallon sat in what the management would consider the least desirable location, a stool chair at the inner end of the bar. From there he couldn't see much of the flaming western sky, but he had a clear view of the piano on the raised dais.

The only problem was, the piano bench was empty. Spicer hadn't put in an appearance yet.

Fallon sipped a draft beer, waiting. There was a closed door in the wall near where he sat that would lead to dressing rooms and offices; the public restrooms were off the lobby outside. When Spicer finally showed, he would probably make his entrance through that door.

Only he didn't show.

6:15.

6:30.

No Spicer.

Fallon finished his beer, motioned to the redheaded woman bartender for another. When she served it, he asked, "Where's the King of the Ivories tonight?"

She didn't seem to know how to answer the question. Finally she said, "He should be here any minute."

"How come he's late?"

"Well, you know," she said vaguely, "delays."

"Sure. Delays."

6:45.

The door in the inner wall opened, but the man who came through wasn't Spicer. Young, plump, wearing a Western-style suit and tie. An agitated frown wrinkled his smooth features when he saw the empty dais. He caught the red-headed bartender's eye, gestured for her to come down, then leaned up close to the bar behind Fallon. The two of them spoke in low tones, but his hearing was acute and he could make out what they were saying.

"Why isn't Courtney here?"

"I don't know, Mr. Haskell. I thought maybe he called in sick."

"He didn't call in at all."

"He's never missed a night or been late before. Maybe he's got the flu or something."

"Too sick to use the telephone? Too drunk is more likely."

"Well, he does like single malt Scotch. But I've never seen him drunk."

Haskell said, "Why do hassles like this always happen on my shift? All right, Tracy, let me know if he comes in," and disappeared through the door.

7:00.

The last of the sunset colors were gone and darkness had begun its descent. The evening star grew bright to the east in the clear purple-black sky. People came into the lounge, people went out. None of them was Court Spicer.

Fallon was on edge now. If Spicer wasn't sick or drunk, if he had spooked and gone on the run again, finding Kevin would be a hell of a lot more difficult, if not impossible. He didn't want to think what Casey might do if that happened.

7:15.

The inner door opened. Haskell again, looking flustered and angry now. He motioned Tracy down and leaned toward her over the bar, once more within Fallon's hearing.

"Still a no-show," she said.

"Damn these musicians. You can't depend on any of them. I called his cell number and it went straight to voice mail."

"Should we make an announcement? Some of the customers have been asking about him."

"Not just yet," Haskell said. "Give him another fifteen or twenty minutes. And give me a Wild Turkey on the rocks."

Haskell stayed put at the bar with his drink, glancing at his watch every three or four minutes and scowling. Just past 7:30, he went back through the door—to make another call to Spicer's cell, Fallon thought. He was gone less than five minutes.

"Still not here and still no answer on his cell phone," he said to Tracy. "If it's up to me, he'll be looking for another job tomorrow."

She said, "Maybe we ought to send somebody out to check on him."

"Oh, sure. Who? I'm not about to drive all the way out to Bullhead City. Go ahead and make the announcement."

Fallon thought: What the hell, give it a shot. He swiveled his stool chair to face the night shift manager. "I couldn't help overhearing," he said. "I've been waiting for Courtney myself, and not to listen to his music."

"Yes?" Haskell gave him a half-appraising, half-distracted look.

"My name's Jackson, Sam Jackson. I own a half interest in a club in Vegas. So happens Steve Courtney played with a trio at my place a while back."

"Is that right?"

"I heard he had a gig here and I drove down to see him. I've got a business proposition he might be interested in."

"What, a better job offer?"

"Not exactly. I don't raid other establishments."

"Yes, well, you can see that he's not here and more than an hour and a half late. It's not likely he'll show tonight."

"That's too bad," Fallon said. "I need to talk to him as soon as possible. You're not going to send someone out to see if he's home?"

"No."

"Well, how about if I do it and let you know? I'm tired of just sitting around waiting. Only thing is, I'll need his address. I don't know where he lives."

Haskell looked at him steadily for about ten seconds. Then, "What's the name of the place you own in Vegas, Mr. Jackson?"

"Own a half interest in. The Star Lounge." It was the first name that came into Fallon's head. "On Flamingo."

"Wait here."

Haskell disappeared again through the door. Going to his office to check up on Sam Jackson? If that was it, Fallon could maneuver his way out of the Star Lounge lie, but he wouldn't get the address. Long shot anyway. But worth it under the circumstances.

Haskell was back—too quickly for him to have done any checking. Fallon relaxed, keeping his expression neutral. He was about to get lucky after all.

"Courtney lives at 60 Desert Rose Lane in Bullhead City," Haskell said. "I'm afraid I can't tell you where that is or how to get there."

"No problem. My car has GPS."

Haskell handed him a card. "My office number is on there. Let me know, will you? Or if you find Courtney, tell him to call me. And he'd better have a damn good excuse."

"I'll do all I can to track him down, Mr. Haskell. You can count on that."

In the Jeep on the way up Casino Drive he called Casey's cell number to tell her why he'd been delayed, that he'd gotten Spicer's address. But she didn't answer. Why would she have her phone switched off? Accident, maybe, or because she was trying to get some rest. She was expecting him to come back there, not to call.

Behind him to the north, as he crossed the bridge into Arizona, the carnival dazzle of lights and neon colors cast by the Laughlin casinos stained the night sky, turned the surface of the Colorado into a distorted reflector dominated by crimson, as if the river had been fouled with currents of blood. By comparison, Bullhead City seemed sedately lit. There wasn't much traffic over here. Monday evening quiet. All the night action, all the noise, belonged to the Nevada side.

The Jeep's GPS led him down Highway 95 to Silver Creek Road, then through a series of secondary streets into a housing development so new that some homes were still under construction. Sunrise Acres, according to a sign—the same tract that Co-River Management had featured in its wall decorations. Stucco-and-tile-roofed homes of various sizes on large lots. Even out here in desert country, lease and rental prices would be substantial. Spicer wouldn't be able to afford one of these places on the scale salary the Wagonwheel paid a lounge act. His high-living expenses had to be underwritten by David Rossi.

Desert Rose Lane was a short dead-end street, three two-story houses on each side. A couple of them looked as though they might be unoccupied, and only two of the others showed lights, the first on the left coming in, the second on the right at the far end.

Fallon relaxed a little when he saw that number 60 was the lighted one at the end. Somebody was there, Spicer or possibly a guard on Kevin; the lights, and the bulky shape of an SUV in the driveway, told him that.

He parked in front of the dark house next door. Before leaving the motel earlier, he'd locked the unloaded Ruger in the console storage compartment; he took it out, slid it inside his belt under the light jacket he wore. A loaded weapon, even if you didn't intend to use it, was a foolish risk with a young boy on the premises. Running a bluff with an unloaded gun went against his army training, but if taking action was necessary, it was better than relying solely on hand-to-hand combat techniques. Whoever was inside the house wasn't likely to answer the door packing heat.

He locked the Jeep, walked slowly to number 60. The spicy scent of sage was strong in the warm darkness. The first thing he saw as he neared the front porch was the thin wedge of light that lay across the tiles. It came through a crack between the door and the jamb: the door was open inward a few inches. Funny. Why leave it open like that, even in what was probably a safe neighborhood?

The doorbell was a vertical strip of lighted plastic; Fallon pushed it and listened to chimes roll out within. Half a minute passed with no response. He thumbed the strip again. Still no response.

He leaned close to the crack in the door. The silence inside and out now seemed acute, charged. He could feel the muscles across his shoulders pulling together, knotting—the same physical reaction he'd had that time in Cochise County, before kicking in the door of a hotel room where a drunken soldier had been holding a woman against her will.

One more push on the doorbell. When that didn't bring anybody, he drew the Ruger and used the back of his left hand to nudge the door open halfway. Foyer, palely lit by a suspended fixture. He leaned his head inside and called out, "Courtney! Steve Courtney!"

The words echoed faintly, died into more heavy silence.

Enter uninvited and technically he'd be committing criminal trespass. But the door was open and it shouldn't be, and the lights were on and they shouldn't be if there was nobody in the house. He couldn't just walk away now.

He called the Courtney name again, then went in and nudged the door closed with his shoulder.

The living room and dining room that opened off of the foyer were both fully furnished. Lease or rental, maybe even one of the tract's original model homes. As often as Spicer traveled from gig to gig, he wouldn't have bought a place like this if he could have afforded it.

Fallon moved cautiously through the downstairs rooms. No sign of anybody. But when he went upstairs to where the bedrooms were, into the hall that bisected the house—

Man on the hallway floor.

Fallon stopped, staring down at him. The back of his scalp crawled.

Dead man. Curled up fetally on his side, both hands pressed under his sternum. Blood and scorch marks on his white shirtfront. Eyes open and staring sightlessly, mouth in a rictus, blood and dried spittle staining the dyed brown goatee.

Court Spicer.

FOUR

Fallon's first thought was of the boy. He ran along the hall, shouldering open doors and flicking lights on briefly to scan the interiors. The door standing ajar at the far end had a pair of hasps screwed to it and its frame, an open padlock and a key on a chain hanging from one. A bedside lamp was lit inside, but the room, like all the others, was empty.

Kevin's room.

Kevin's prison cell.

Single bed, nightstand, dresser, TV set. Bookcase with a row of thick paperback books. The only window shuttered and padlocked and probably nailed down. Signs of hasty packing: dresser drawers pulled out, closet mostly empty, a couple of items of boys' clothing forgotten on the floor.

Gone. Taken away by whoever killed Spicer.

Fallon ran back to where the dead man lay, dropped to one knee without touching him. Shock still had hold of him. He'd seen corpses before; you can't grow up in East L.A. and spend four years as an army MP, even on stateside duty, without coming face-to-face with violent death. But this was something outside his experience, as inexplicable as it was unexpected.

Spicer had been shot once at close range. Small-caliber weapon, maybe a .22. What blood had leaked out of the wound was tacky, drying. In addition to the white shirt, he wore trousers and a knotted tie—his Sunset Lounge outfit except for the jacket. Dressed and ready to leave when whoever shot him showed up. That and the drying blood put the time of death at between five and five-thirty. Three hours.

Who? Why? And why take Kevin? To liberate him from his father, or because he was a witness to the shooting?

Fallon stood up and leaned against the wall. Training and instinct urged him to notify the police immediately. Right thing to do, start them looking for the boy as soon as possible. For his own protection, too, even though Casey could verify his whereabouts when Spicer died.

But not just yet.

His first obligation was to Casey: she had to be told about this, and by him, not the law. In person was better, but there wasn't time for that. He hit the redial button on his cell phone.

No answer. Her cell was still switched off.

Dammit! He didn't know the motel number . . . wait, yes he did. The letterhead receipt for the two rooms he'd paid for by credit card. He found it in his pocket, called the number, asked the clerk for Casey's room.

Ten empty rings.

That made him even edgier. She should be in the room, waiting for him. And if she'd gone out for some reason, why hadn't she made sure her cell phone was turned on? Where was she?

The need for movement drove him into the bedroom nearest to where the body lay. It was the one Spicer had been using; his dark blue dinner jacket was on a hanger on the closet door, his wallet in an inside pocket. Fallon eased the wallet out, fanned through it. Two hundred dollars in twenties and tens. No credit cards—Spicer must have paid for everything in cash. No union card. The only ID was a Nevada driver's license in the name of Steven Courtney. Bought and paid for, probably in Vegas and probably from Bobby J. or one of his cronies.

Fallon wiped the wallet with a hand towel from the adjacent bathroom, returned it to the coat pocket. Then he used the towel to open drawers in a small writing desk. Looking for blackmail evidence, anything that might explain the shooting. All he found was a few receipts for meals and minor purchases. The closet and the dresser contained clothing, most of it on the expensive side, and little else. The nightstand was empty except for a package of condoms and a prostitute's full-color business card like the ones they handed out on the Vegas Strip.

He was sweating now, despite the air-conditioned coolness. Without touching anything, he made a quick search of the other bedrooms, then went downstairs and prowled the first-floor rooms. The place had a static, unlived-in feel; the only personal items Spicer had brought to it were in the two upstairs bedrooms.

He made another call to Casey's room at the motel. Still no answer.

Where the hell *was* she?

He'd been in there with the dead man a long time now—too long. Call the police, get it over with. Worry about Casey later.

He couldn't make himself do it.

The urgency he felt now was to find her, find out what had gone wrong at the motel; she was still his first priority. Bring her back here with him, let her wait in the Jeep while he discovered the body all over again, and then he'd call in the law. Self-protection for both of them. There was time to do it that way, and not too much risk: the chance that anybody in the lighted neighboring house had seen him come in here was fairly slim.

He thought about shutting off the lights before leaving, but he didn't do it. If he hadn't been seen coming in, he'd be careful not to be seen going out. And you don't alter or compromise a crime scene in any way if you can avoid it. The door lock was a deadbolt, so he was able to close the door without setting it. From the porch, he made sure the street was empty before crossing to the Jeep.

The same thought kept running on a loop inside his head: leaving like this is a mistake—you know damn well it is. But it hadn't stopped him inside and it didn't stop him now.

The drive to the motel took twenty long minutes. He had to keep telling himself to take it easy, observe the speed limit, do nothing to call attention to himself.

No lights showed behind the curtained window in Casey's unit. Fallon put the Jeep into an empty space, went to rap on the door and call her name.

Silence. He knocked again, louder, and a third time before he gave it up and trotted down to the motel office.

The night clerk was a college-age kid with a scraggly crescent of chin whiskers. Fallon said, "My friend, the woman I checked in with, should be in her room but she doesn't answer the door." He described her, gave her room number. "Do you know if she went out?"

"No, sir. I haven't seen anyone looks like that."

"She might still be in the room. Sick or something. Could you open it up so I can check?"

"Well, I don't know . . . You say she's a friend of yours?"

Fallon dragged the receipt out of his pocket, slapped it down. "I paid for both rooms, you can see that. I'm worried about her. Come on, get your passkey. It won't take long."

The clerk didn't argue. They went to Casey's room and he keyed open the door and put on the lights. Fallon pushed around him, inside. Empty. There was a measure of relief in that, but none in the fact that her suitcase and overnight bag were also missing.

He took a quick look around, thinking that she might have left a note. Nothing. The only signs that she'd ever been there were the rumpled bed and a towel on the bathroom floor.

Outside he asked the clerk, "How long have you been here tonight?"

"Since five o'clock."

"On the desk the whole time? You didn't go out for some reason and turn it over to somebody else?"

"No, sir. I've been here the whole time. If your friend had checked out, she would have had to do it with me."

"She wouldn't have checked out," Fallon said.

"Well, she'll probably be back. Maybe she just went out somewhere to eat."

Fallon didn't answer that. He said a curt thanks, unlocked the door to his own room, and closed himself inside.

Immediately he tried her cell number again. Out of service.

Spicer murdered, the boy missing again, and now this. There must be some connection, but what? None of it made any sense. Casey had no reason to leave voluntarily . . . unless she was the one who'd killed Spicer and taken Kevin. Was that even remotely possible? He didn't see how it could be. She'd have had to find out somehow where they were living and then get out there in a cab right after Fallon left for the Wagonwheel. There might have been time for her to do that, barely—he could be wrong about the time of death—and the weapon could have belonged to Spicer and she'd managed to get it away from him . . .

No, Christ, he didn't buy it for a second. She was emotional, unpredictable, with self-destructive tendencies, but he couldn't picture her as homicidal. And she wasn't crazy, which she'd have to be to want revenge badly enough to jeopardize her relationship with her son.

The only other possibility he could think of was that whoever killed Spicer had kidnapped both the boy and Casey. But how would the shooter know where she was staying? Well, there was an answer to that: she'd been seen and recognized at some point today, or he had, and they'd been followed here the way he'd followed Bobby J. last night. But then how would the follower know she was here alone? The timing said he'd have had to be in Bullhead City when Fallon left for the Sunset Lounge. An accomplice staked out here? Bobby J. and Yellow Beard working together?

Far-fetched. Unbelievable.

He quit trying to make sense of it, focused instead on what he was going to do. Drive back to the Bullhead City house, refind the body, call the law? Still an option, but not a good one with Casey missing. Without her he couldn't prove he'd been here until 5:40 tonight, and his reasons for hunting Spicer might seem suspicious without corroboration. Like as not, with no other handy suspects, they'd chuck his ass into jail and hold him as a material witness. And if they wanted to, they could build a pretty good circumstantial case against him. The thought of spending even a short time behind bars put a cold knot in his gut. You couldn't get any farther from wide open spaces than a jail cell.

Could he get away with not reporting the murder? Maybe, if he was lucky. A lot of people knew he'd been looking for Spicer, but he'd never once used his own name and most of the inquiries had been in Vegas. The only ones in Laughlin who knew were the two women at Co-River Management and the night shift manager at the Sunset Lounge. They could describe him, but that was all and it wasn't much. There was nothing distinctive or memorable about his looks. Average. His description fit ten thousand other guys.

The manager, Haskell, would remember giving him Steven Courtney's address and probably pass that information on to the police. But there was a way for Fallon to cover himself on that, up to a point.

The card Haskell had given him was in his shirt pocket; he fished it out, punched up the number. While it was ringing, he had a few bad seconds trying to remember the phony name he'd used, finally retrieved it just before Haskell came on the line.

"This is Sam Jackson, Mr. Haskell, the lounge owner from Vegas. Has Steven Courtney shown up or called in?"

"Neither one. You didn't find him, I take it?"

"Afraid not. His car is in his driveway, but the house is dark and nobody answers the door. I thought maybe he'd finally shown up there. Now . . . well, he's out of luck on that business matter I was telling you about. I'm heading back to Vegas early tomorrow morning."

"He's out of luck here, too," Haskell said. "If you want to hire him, he'll be available come tomorrow."

"No, thanks. I don't want no-show performers working for me any more than you do."

Okay. Covered at least until the police checked on Sam Jackson and found out he and the Star Lounge didn't exist.

How long before somebody found Spicer's body? It might be days; no one from the Wagonwheel was likely to go out there to check on him. And when the body was discovered, the victim was Steven Courtney, according to his driver's license and everybody who'd known him down here. In a homicide case the law usually checked the victim's fingerprints, but there was a chance small-town law might not bother, and if they did, that Spicer's fingerprints weren't on file anywhere. A chance that the law would never connect Steven Courtney and Court Spicer until somebody made the connection for them.

So time was on Fallon's side. Enough time to find out what had happened to Casey and her son.

Final decision made, right or wrong. He was in too deep to get out of this mess any other way. Besides, she was still his responsibility. Quit on her now and he'd be quitting on himself.

Fallon gathered his gear, stowed it in the Jeep, checked out. Casey still hadn't contacted him. Wouldn't or couldn't. Wherever she was, wherever the boy was, it wasn't Laughlin or Bullhead City.

Five minutes later he was on Highway 95, heading north. He had to start someplace, and the best and closest option was Vegas.

PART IV
LAS VEGAS

ONE

CASEY'S TOYOTA WAS STILL in long-term parking at McCarran International.

That didn't have to mean anything one way or another. He'd driven straight to the airport, exceeding the speed limit most of the way; the probable window of time of her disappearance from the Laughlin motel was not much more than three hours. If she'd left on her own for some reason, it might not be easy for her to get to Vegas to claim the car.

He was dog-tired from the day's stress and all the miles he'd put on the Jeep. It was close to midnight now. Not much he could do at this hour. Number one on his list of possibilities was Bobby J., and trying to brace a hardcase when he wasn't thinking clearly and his reactions were sluggish would be a mistake.

Another motel, this one closer to McCarran than the previous Best Western. Five hours' rest should be plenty; as soon as he was in bed he set the digital alarm clock on the nightstand. But the tension wouldn't ease enough to let him sleep right away. Every time he shut his eyes, he could see Spicer lying there dead in the hall, and the padlock on the door to Kevin's room, and the items of kid's clothing dropped and forgotten on the floor.

Seven thirty, Tuesday morning. McCarran International, long-term parking garage.

The Toyota was still there.

*   *   *

Number one on the list: Bobby J.

It didn't take much imagination to picture a man with his track record shooting Spicer—money, a falling-out of some kind, whatever reason— and then snatching the only witness. What Fallon still couldn't figure was Casey. If Bobby J. had grabbed her too, how and why? The only way it added up was that she'd somehow learned Spicer's address on her own, made a wrong-headed decision to take a cab to Bullhead City, and been at the rented house when Spicer was shot.

Two witnesses, if that was the explanation. And then what? Two more killings—a woman and a young boy, in cold blood?

Don't go there, Fallon. Get it out of your head.

Bobby J.

And no pussyfooting around this time. Straight at him. Fast and hard.

The house at 246 Sandstone Way had a run-down look by daylight. Scarred stucco facade, weeds in the yard, the big prickly pear cactus grown into a wild tangle of branches, thorny pads, and unpicked fruit. The driveway was empty. No sign of the Mustang on the street, either. But that didn't have to mean nobody was home.

Fallon drove on by, parked around the corner. He'd taken the Ruger out of the console storage space last night, put it back again this morning. The difference was that now it held six live rounds. The risk of carrying a loaded weapon was no greater now than the risk he'd taken in not reporting Spicer's murder, leaving the scene and the area. And it would be stupid to go up against a man like Bobby J. without it.

He tucked the weapon into his waistband, above his right hip, and got out and walked back to 246. A young, plump woman in a housedress was picking up her newspaper on the property next door; she glanced at him curiously as he passed by. He nodded, smiling, keeping it casual. She didn't smile back. And she lingered to watch him as he moved on up the front walk and rang Bobby J.'s doorbell.

Nobody answered.

He tried again. Echoes in an empty house.

Shit. All worked up for a confrontation, and now this. He felt like slamming his fist into the wall to relieve the pressure.

The neighbor was still standing there looking at him. He went back to the sidewalk and over into her yard, still keeping it casual, putting on another smile for her. She glared at him in return—a look that managed to convey a combination of weariness, annoyance, and suspicion.

"Hold it right there, Mister," she said before he reached her. "If you're selling something this early in the day . . ."

"I'm not a salesman."

"You a friend of that pair?"

"No. I have some business with Bobby J."

"Bobby J." Her tone and her mobile face both reflected distaste. "You don't look like one of his kind."

"What kind is that?"

"Sleazebag."

"I don't know him. I'm just a man trying to do a job."

Screeches and other child noises came from inside her house, deepening her scowl. "Damn kids," she said. "I should've had my tubes tied after the first one."

Fallon said, "Does he own the house over there?"

"Who? Bobby Jackoff and his slut?"

"Jackoff?"

"That's what my husband calls him. Some Polish name."

"What name?"

"Don't you know, you have business with him?"

"All I know is Bobby J."

"Jackowsky, Jabowski . . . no . . . Jablonsky. That's it, Jablonsky."

"About the house. Does he own it?"

"Leased. The slut lived there before he moved in last year."

"Candy?"

The woman made a spitting mouth. "Candy Barr. With two r's. My God, the names these women give themselves."

"Can you tell me what time they left this morning?"

"For all I know," she said, "neither of 'em was home all night. It wouldn't be the first time. Quiet over there for a change."

"You didn't see his car?"

"Didn't see it, didn't hear him jazzing the engine like he does some mornings. Or when he comes home drunk or stoned in the middle of the night when decent people are trying to sleep. I can't tell you how many times he's woken up the kids. They get woken up, I don't get any sleep, my husband doesn't get any sleep."

"Do you know if he has a job?"

"A job? Him? Hah. He does anything at all besides gamble, it's probably something crooked."

"He's a gambler?"

"Poker. Big poker player, to hear him tell it. Bragged to my husband once about how much money he wins at the casinos."

"Any one in particular?"

"Who knows? The one where Candy Barr works, probably. Calls herself a dancer. Hooker, more likely. Foul mouth. You should hear the things they shout at each other over there. You should've heard what she called *me* once. It's enough to make you sick to your stomach."

"There's a friend of Bobby J.'s—big man, blond, thick blond beard. Drives a Ford Explorer."

"Oh, him. He comes around sometimes. Another sleazebag."

"You know his name?"

"No, and I don't want to know it." She frowned at Fallon. "You sure ask a lot of questions."

Before he could make up a response, more screeches rose from inside her house, followed by a long wailing shriek. A girl about five came running out in her pajamas, yowling. "Mommy, Mommy, Conner hit me, he hit me with a *spoon*, he *hurt* me!"

"I'll hurt him," the woman said grimly. "I'll blister his little ass for him."

"Blister his ass, blister his ass!"

"Shut your mouth. You sound like the slut next door." She took the little girl's hand, led her inside without another word to Fallon.

* * *

Casino Slot Machine Repair was open for business when Fallon pulled into the lot. The only vehicle parked there was a van with the name of the business lettered on the sides. He slotted the Jeep next to it, went inside to the offkey clang of a bell above the door.

Cluttered showroom, heavy with the smell of machine oil. Rows of electronic and mechanical slots and video poker machines lined two walls. Restored and for sale, according to placards on each, their cases polished, their glassed-in faces making the room bright with color even though they were unlit. A combination workroom and warehouse, visible through an open set of doors, took up most of the rear of the building—the place where Bobby J. and Yellow Beard had waited in ambush.

A man in overalls, wiping his hands on a greasy towel, appeared from the workroom. Midforties, fair-haired, clean-shaven except for a Fu Manchu mustache. And big—almost as big as Yellow Beard. He looked at Fallon in a neutral way before he said, "Sam Vinson, at your service. What can I do for you? Repair problem?"

"No. I—"

"Looking to buy, then? I just finished restoring a real nice '64 Bally Star Special, one of the first electro-mechanical hopper pay slots. Perfect condition. Make you a good price on it."

"No thanks. I'm looking for Bobby Jablonsky."

"Bobby J.?" Nothing changed in Vinson's expression. "Well, then, you've come to the wrong place. Jablonsky don't work here."

"Friend of yours, though, isn't he?"

"Not me. My brother Clem."

Clem Vinson—Yellow Beard. The resemblance was plain enough. "Clem work here with you?"

"Sometimes. Not today."

"Where would I find him?"

"At his other job, probably. Golden Horseshoe in Glitter Gulch. Maintenance staff."

"I hear Bobby J. plays some poker at the Golden Horseshoe."

"*Some* poker? He's a hound, man—always in a Texas Hold 'Em game, day or night. Clem, too, when he can afford it." Vinson paused, as if he'd had a sudden thought. "Say, you wouldn't be a bill collector?"

"Not me. No way."

"Then how come you're so interested in Bobby J.?"

Fallon gave him the business proposition line, and Vinson laughed. "Well, if there's money in it, Bobby J.'s your man. He's open to just about anything that'll support his poker habit."

"So I've heard."

"Oh, yeah," Vinson said, soberly this time. "Just about anything at all."

In the Jeep, Fallon tried Casey's cell number again. Still out of service.

He called her home number in San Diego. No answer.

Vernon Young Realty would be open by now. He called there, on the chance that Vernon Young had heard from Casey, but the woman he spoke to said Mr. Young was out of the office. She didn't know when he would return.

He called Young's home number. Answering machine.

He listened again to the brief, anxious message from Sharon Rossi, left on his voice mail while he was talking to Sam Vinson. She hadn't heard from him, would he please call her as soon as possible?

Yes, but not yet. Not just yet.

The Golden Horseshoe's Poker Room, like the rest of the casino, had a Western motif—loosely patterned after the standard saloon sets in old TV shows like *Gunsmoke* or *Bonanza*. Green baize tables, crystal chandeliers, a long brass-railed bar with the painting of a nude on the wall above it. Strategically placed spittoons. Smoke-filled air. The soft pile carpeting and leather chairs spoiled the effect, but that was Vegas for you: all illusion, but none of it quite what it was intended to be. Elaborate, ornate, and phony as hell.

This early in the day, only two of the tables had players. Omaha and Texas Hold 'Em games. Four men, one woman at the Texas Hold 'Em table. Fallon quick-scanned the men there and those at the other table as he walked by. Bobby J. wasn't one of them; neither was Clem Vinson.

He asked the bartender if Bobby J. had been in today. Head wag, and a bored "Haven't seen him."

"What time does he usually show up?"

"Couldn't tell you, Mister. They come, they go, they win, they lose. I just pour the drinks."

Fallon turned into the Denny's parking lot next to the Rest-a-While, parked toward the rear—out of sight of the motel office. There was a low retaining wall behind the ell on that side; he climbed over it, keeping his face averted just in case Max Arbogast happened to be looking out. Eight or nine cars occupied the room spaces, none of them a Mustang. He went straight to number 20, but even before he got there he knew this was another bust. A maid's cart stood next to the open door of the adjacent unit and the whine of a vacuum cleaner came from inside. If Jablonsky had been hosting one of his drug parties for underage girls, the maid wouldn't have been allowed in the vicinity.

He was tempted to brace Arbogast again, but what would that buy him except the satisfaction of making the little bastard squirm? Arbogast wasn't close to Bobby J.; he wouldn't know where to find him on short notice. But he'd be on the phone trying to find him five seconds after Fallon left.

Another drive-by on Sandstone Way. No Mustang or other vehicle on the property. No Bobby J., no Candy.

Time to shift gears. It was early yet; take care of his other business, then come back to Jablonsky afterward.

He parked around the corner and returned Sharon Rossi's call. As soon as he identified himself, she said, "I've been waiting and waiting to hear from you. Have you located Spicer yet?"

"Not on the phone, Mrs. Rossi."

"Then you have? Can't you just tell me if—"

"In person. Are you home?"

"Yes, but—"

"I can be there in half an hour."

". . . You're back in Las Vegas, then."

"That's right."

"We can't meet here," she said. "My husband came home this morning, he's here now resting."

"What time did he come home?"

"About two hours ago."

"Where did he go on his business trip?"

"Where he usually goes. Chemco's plant in Phoenix."

Phoenix. Only a little more than two hundred miles south of Laughlin. Fast, easy drive up and back in a rental car. There were also feeder flights between Sky Harbor International and the Laughlin-Bullhead City airport.

Fallon said, "I'll want to talk to him too."

"What? My God, what for?"

"Some questions that need answering."

"About Spicer?" Her voice had risen a couple of octaves. "You're not going to tell David about our arrangement? You can't, he'll be furious with me . . ."

"You just let me handle it, Mrs. Rossi. I'll keep you out of it as much as I can."

"But I don't understand. What have you found out? Why won't you—"

"Half an hour," Fallon said, and broke the connection.

TWO

THE GATES AT THE foot of the desert mesa were open, evidently left that way for him by Sharon Rossi. She was outside waiting when he drove onto the packed-sand parking area, came hurrying over as he stepped out of the Jeep. Dressed all in white again—peasant blouse, pleated skirt, sandals—but she didn't look cool or self-possessed today. Anxiety had cut thin furrows into her artfully made-up face. There was angry determination in her, too; you could see it in the pinched corners of her mouth, the tightly set jawline.

One other thing he noticed: the all-white outfit was loose-fitting, but not loose enough to conceal a handgun, even one as small as the .32 purse job she'd showed him on Sunday. She might have had it strapped to her thigh under the skirt, but he didn't think so; she wasn't the type. He'd have to watch her inside, though: the automatic could be stashed somewhere for easy access. He wasn't taking chances with anybody now, not where weapons were concerned.

She said, "So you're here. Now tell me what you found out."

Fallon ignored that. "Where's your husband?"

"In our bedroom, dressing. He's going to his office."

"Did you tell him I was coming?"

"No. Not without some idea of what's going on. I won't be blindsided on this, Mr. Fallon, not in my own home."

"It won't happen like that."

"So you say. *Did* you find Court Spicer?"

He was going to gamble here too, cautiously, as he'd been prepared all day to do with Bobby Jablonsky. It was the only way he was likely to get fast and honest answers.

He said, "Yes. I found him."

"The evidence we discussed? His hold over my husband?"

"No. But that may not be an issue now."

"What does that mean, not an issue?"

"I need to know some things before we go inside. Did you contact Co-River Management yourself yesterday?"

The question caught her off-stride. "I don't . . . no, of course not."

"Find out where Spicer's been living any other way?"

"No. How would I?"

"Where were you last night?"

". . . Why do you want to know that?"

"Just answer the question."

"Here. Right here."

"Alone?"

"No. Lupe, our housekeeper, was home—she lives with us."

"Is she here now?"

"No. I sent her out to do some shopping."

He'd been watching her closely. All he saw was anxious bewilderment.

"All right, let's go in. Tell your husband I have some important personal business to discuss with him. If you want to say I was here on Sunday, that's up to you."

"What are you going to say to him?"

"Depends on what he has to say to me. Either way, I won't embarrass you."

"You'd better not," she said coldly. "I trusted you—don't betray that trust."

Inside, she took him into the sunken living room and left him there. The drapes were open over the windows overlooking the courtyard; sunlight streaming in laid bright gold patches across the tile floor. Fallon paced a little, waiting. Five minutes, no more, before he heard footsteps and Sharon Rossi brought her husband in.

David Rossi was in his late forties, lanky, with thinning brush-cut hair and a long-chinned, ruddy, freshly shaven face. The expression on it now was flat and neutral; if he played poker, he was probably good at it. He wore a light-colored suit and tie, expensive and perfectly tailored—the kind of outfit the high-level execs at Unidyne paraded around in. Corporate badges of success and power.

Rossi said brusquely, without offering to shake hands, "I don't know you, Mr . . . Fallon, is it?"

"That's right."

"Personal business, my wife said. What does that mean, exactly?"

"Court Spicer."

Rossi closed up, tight. You could see it happening, like watching a desert cactus flower fold its petals at sunset. But the poker face revealed nothing of what was happening behind it. He looked at Fallon, hard, for several seconds. Then he looked at his wife.

"Sharon," he said, "please leave us alone."

She said, "No. I want to hear what he has to say."

"Sharon . . ."

"I know about Court Spicer, David."

"You know? What do you know?"

"That you've been paying him money. That he has some kind of hold over you. I'm not blind and I'm not stupid."

Rossi said, "Oh Lord," in a low, pained voice. Then, with a flare of anger, "Dammit, we're not alone here."

"I already knew about it," Fallon said.

"You . . . How? How did you know?"

Sharon Rossi gave Fallon a look of appeal. He said, "It doesn't matter how I found out."

"What are you, another bloodsucker? Is that why you're here?"

"No."

"Spicer. Did he send you?"

"Nobody sent me."

"Then why? What do you want? Who are you?"

"A friend of Spicer's ex-wife. He kidnapped their son four months ago."

"He . . . what?"

"You didn't know that?"

"I didn't even know he had a son."

"Eight and a half years old. The mother had custody and Spicer kidnapped him. I've been helping her try to find him."

"My God. He's an even worse bastard than I thought."

"The last time you saw him was when?"

"A week, two weeks, I don't remember exactly."

"A week ago Sunday," his wife said. "The last big jam."

"Yes, that's right."

Fallon said, "He came with a big man with a dragon tattoo on his right wrist. You remember him?"

"Yes, but I don't know who he is. I never saw him before. A lot of people come to my jams, they bring others with them . . ."

"Have you talked to Spicer since then?"

"No."

"You know he's been living in the Laughlin area?"

"Yes."

"Where, exactly? His address?"

"No."

"Sure about that?"

"You think he'd let me have his address? Not if you know him, you don't. A mail drop, that's all he gave me."

"Where were you between five and eight last night, Mr. Rossi?"

Rossi said stiffly, "Why are you asking all these questions? What do you want from me?"

"Answer the last one and I'll tell you."

Sharon Rossi said, "Answer him, David."

"I was in Phoenix," he said. "A business engagement. Drinks at five, dinner at seven. There were five of us. Would you like their names?"

A man with Rossi's money and corporate status could get five people to lie for him if he needed to, but Fallon didn't think he was lying. Now was the time to make sure. Pull the pin on a verbal grenade.

He said, "Spicer's dead."

The explosion rocked them both. Shock is one of the hardest things to fake; the open mouths and staring eyes were genuine. The brief silence that followed had a charged quality.

"Dead?" Rossi said numbly. "Dead?"

His wife said, "How? What happened?"

"Somebody killed him last night in the house he was renting."

"Somebody . . . *you*?"

"No, not me. I wouldn't be here telling you about it if I had."

Rossi moved over to one of the leather chairs, started to sit down, changed his mind, and went around and leaned on the back of it. "You thought it was me," he said then.

"I thought it could be," Fallon said. "I don't anymore. Whoever killed him took the boy and maybe the mother too. She was down there with me and she disappeared last night. You might've snatched the boy if he was a homicide witness. I couldn't see any reason why you'd go after the mother, but I had to make sure."

Rossi didn't seem to be listening now. Or to notice when his wife went over next to him and put her hand on his shoulder. His eyes had a unblinking, inward focus. "Dead," he said. "Now I really am screwed."

"David, be quiet."

"They'll find it. They'll come after me."

"Be quiet! You said it yourself—we're not alone."

Rossi said, "He already knows," meaning Fallon.

"No, he doesn't, not everything."

"Screwed. They'll put me in jail. A stupid accident three years ago and I'll go to prison."

Sharon Rossi surprised Fallon by moving backward a step and then slapping her husband across the face, hard. The sound of it was like a pistol shot in the quiet room. Rossi recoiled, lifted a hand to his cheek, stared at her as if he couldn't believe what she'd done.

"All right, then," she said in that coldly angry way of hers. "Go ahead, tell us both. What stupid accident? What did you do?"

Rossi shook his head, but it wasn't a refusal. Under that cool corporate façade, the man had a conscience that had been giving him hell for a long time. You could see it in his eyes, the grayish pallor that had replaced the ruddiness. Whatever he'd done, he was haunted by it.

Sharon Rossi sensed it too. She glanced at Fallon, an unreadable look this time, then fixed her gaze on her husband again. "I'm tired of all the secrets and evasions, David. I have a right to know. Did you hurt somebody? Kill somebody? *What?*"

"It wasn't my fault."

"What wasn't your fault?"

Rossi didn't answer until she jabbed him with the heel of her hand. Then he said in a halting voice, like a man confessing a mortal sin to a priest, "I had too much to drink that night, I don't remember everything that happened. The woman . . . dark street . . . all of a sudden right there in my headlights, running like somebody was chasing her . . . *she* must have been drunk. I couldn't stop in time. I swear to God it wasn't my fault."

"Hit and run," Sharon Rossi said. "You hit some woman and then drove away without reporting it."

"God help me, yes."

"Did you even stop to see how badly she was hurt?"

"I stopped. She was . . . there wasn't anything we could do. He said we had to get out of there before somebody came. I was confused, scared . . . I let him talk me into it."

"Spicer. He was in the car with you?"

"There was a jam in South Vegas. I went alone, you didn't want to go. It was late, four A.M., when it broke up. Spicer was there, he asked me for a ride to his hotel . . . Lord, if only I'd said no . . ."

"You obviously had the damage to the car fixed. If he'd gone to the police later, it would have been your word against his. Unless he had some kind of evidence. Did he?"

"Yes. Photographs. He took them with his cell phone camera. The woman, the blood, the damage, my license plate." Rossi drew in a shuddery breath. "The police are sure to find them now that he's dead . . ."

"Not necessarily. It depends on where he kept them." Sharon Rossi's ice-gray eyes shifted to pin Fallon. "You know Spicer's dead—if you didn't kill him, that means you found him. Did you find anything else?"

"There wasn't anything else to find."

"You're sure there were no photographs?"

"Not anywhere you'd think to look."

"Did you notify the police that Spicer was dead?"

Fallon said nothing.

"No, you didn't," she said. "And you won't say anything about a three-year-old accident, either, will you? Without evidence it would be your word against David's and mine. You know that as well as I do."

"I know it."

"So you're going to forget what you just heard and let my husband and me handle it. In return, we'll forget you told us Spicer is dead and you didn't report finding his body. Deal?"

He didn't have any choice. He'd satisfied himself that neither of them had anything to do with Spicer's death, but he'd overestimated his ability to control the situation, let himself get backed into a moral corner. Maybe the police would find those photographs and maybe they wouldn't; maybe David Rossi would continue to get away with a drunken, fatal hit-and-run. Either way there wasn't a damn thing Fallon could do about it.

"Deal," he said.

THREE

H E DIDN'T LIKE HIMSELF much when he left the Rossi hacienda. Getting in deeper and deeper with every move he made. But it was too late for him to quit, even if he ended up hating himself. All he could think about was Casey and her son, out there somewhere, alive—they had to be alive. Nobody else was hunting for them. They didn't have anybody else.

Hey, Geena, he thought, how do you like this for a commitment? What would you say if you knew about it?

Well, he had a pretty good idea what she'd say. Something like "This isn't a commitment anymore, it's an obsession." Something like "You're not as tough as you think you are." Something like "Fools rush in. You're a damned fool, Rick." And she'd be right, according to her view of him and the world she lived in.

But she'd be wrong, too. He might be a damned fool, but living in his world depended on finishing what he'd started.

The Rossis were out of it now. Bobby Jablonsky was still his last best hope in Vegas. All he had to do was find him.

He made another trip to Sandstone Way. Still nobody there.

Where was Jablonsky? Somewhere down in the Laughlin area? Candy should be home, even if he wasn't. One o'clock now. Maybe she'd gone to the Golden Horseshoe early. Maybe Bobby J. was there playing poker by now.

Wrong on both counts. Neither of them was at the casino. Nobody he talked to had seen them yet today.

On the run?

Fallon rejected the thought immediately. From what he knew of the man, Bobby J. wasn't the type to panic. Even the commission of a homicide wouldn't be enough to prod him into running. His dealings with Spicer had been covert; he'd know it was unlikely that he'd come under suspicion once the body was found. He'd just cover his tracks and go on home as if nothing had happened.

He was around Vegas somewhere. Keep looking in the same places and sooner or later he'd turn up.

Midafternoon.

Fallon had been traveling the desert-eater's veins and arteries for nearly three hours, covering the same ground. Sandstone Way, Cheyenne Street and Casino Slot Machine Repair, Glitter Gulch and another quick check-in at the Golden Horseshoe. Still no Bobby J.

His nerves had always been good. Tense situations didn't bother him. If anything, he functioned better under pressure, focused on a single objective. But this was a new experience, more urgent than any except Timmy's fall and fatal injury, and there hadn't been anything he could do about that. Passivity ran against his grain. And that was what all this futile running around amounted to—doing nothing, putting himself and his emotions on hold.

Three thirty-five. Sandstone Way again.

And this time, finally, there was a car in the cracked asphalt driveway.

Not Bobby J.'s Mustang—the light-colored four-door he'd seen parked there on Sunday night.

Candy's wheels.

She took her time answering the door. The reason was that she'd been getting ready for work at the Golden Horseshoe. Putting on makeup: she had a mascara brush in one hand, and she was wearing a thin blue robe with a towel draped around her neck. She scowled at Fallon and said angrily, "What the hell's the idea leaning on the bell like that?"

"Are you Candy Barr?"

"Goddamn salesman," she said, and started to close the door.

He jammed his shoulder and leg against it, shoved hard enough to send her backpedaling. She caught herself as he stepped inside and threw the door shut behind him. He said, "Don't scream. I'm not going to hurt you."

He could have saved his breath; she wasn't the screaming type. A fighter. She came rushing back toward him, her eyes flashing. Her fingernails were long and painted blood-red and she'd have gone straight for his face and eyes if he hadn't shown her the Ruger, drawn the hammer back with an audible click.

It stopped her cold. Her mouth opened, snapped shut. She began to breathe heavily through her nose, staring at the gun.

"What do you want?" The words came out scratchy but with more anger than fear.

"Bobby J."

"Yeah," she said, "that figures. He's not here."

"Where he is?"

"How should I know? I'm not his keeper."

"Anybody else in the house besides you?"

"Nobody else lives here."

"That's not what I asked you."

"No. Just me."

"Let's go make sure."

He moved forward, gesturing with the Ruger. She backed up, finally turned as he came close, and walked away slowly with her head tilted around so she could watch him. The room they were in, the living room, was shabbily furnished but kept neater than he would have expected. The kitchen, a dining alcove, two bedrooms, a bathroom, a utility room, a tiny back porch—all empty. The only one that had a disordered look was the last, the bedroom she shared with Jablonsky: unmade bed, her skimpy costume laid out on it, and a vanity table cluttered with tubes and bottles of makeup.

She said, "You satisfied now?"

"Bobby J. bring anybody here last night?"

"Like who?"

"A woman and a young boy."

"A kid? Bobby J.?" Her laugh was bleak, humorless. "He hates kids."

"I'll bet he does. Answer the question."

"No. The answer is no."

Fallon took a long look at her. Typical Vegas showgirl with the requisite attributes. Midtwenties. Dyed red hair, long and pinned up now for her French can-can routine. The kind of round face and round, top-heavy body that was attractive now but that would run to fat by the time she was forty. The hazel eyes were hard and cynical. Same with the wide mouth. She'd seen a lot and done a lot in her twenty-five years, and not much of it had made her happy. Plaything for users and abusers like Bobby J.

The front of her robe had gaped open, exposing most of one heavy, freckled breast; she made no effort to close it. She saw him looking and misinterpreted his appraisal. "Go ahead and stare, asshole. You try doing anything more, I'll yank your balls out by the roots, gun or no gun."

"Bobby J.'s the rapist, not me."

". . . What's that supposed to mean?"

"Casey Dunbar."

The name bounced right off of her. "Who?"

"So he didn't tell you about his deal with Spicer."

Another bounce. "Who the hell is Spicer?"

"Come on, Candy. Court Spicer—Bobby J. must have mentioned him."

"Bobby J. doesn't tell me his business."

"Unless it has to do with teenage runaways and the Rest-a-While Motel."

". . . I don't know what you're talking about."

Fallon said, "Where was he last night around five o'clock?"

"Why don't you ask him?"

"He wasn't here, was he."

"Who knows? I was working last night. Who *are* you, man? What do you want with Bobby J.?"

"I want to know where he was last night."

"I told you, I don't know. Playing poker. Out trolling for pussy with one of his buddies. Jerking off in the Bellagio lobby. I don't know!"

"Last time you saw him—when?"

"I don't remember. He comes, he goes, I don't keep track."

She wasn't afraid of Fallon, but the Ruger was a hefty piece of artillery and it made her nervous. She kept alternating her gaze between it and him. Deliberately he lowered the hammer, then cocked it again. "When, Candy?"

"Oh, shit, all right. Yesterday around noon."

"He call you any time after that?"

"No."

"Where were you all day?"

"Out eating—I don't cook. Shopping. Getting my hair done. Hanging out with a girlfriend. You think I just sit around here and wait for Bobby J.?"

Fallon said, "There a weapon in the house?"

"Weapon? You mean a gun?"

"That's what I mean."

"No."

"Don't lie to me, Candy. If there's one here, you'd better tell me. Don't make me lock you in a closet and ransack the place to find it."

Her tongue ran a wet circuit of her lips while she made up her mind. "Under the mattress, right side—his side."

The piece was tucked in between the mattress and box springs. Saturday night special, rounds in every chamber. Fallon sniffed the barrel. Not fired recently. Or cleaned recently; there was no odor of gun oil. He emptied the cartridges onto the rumpled top sheet, put the gun back where he'd found it and the loads into his jacket pocket.

"That the only one?"

"One's all you need for protection."

"Sure. Protection. Bobby J. keep another piece in that Mustang of his?"

"No. I don't think so."

"But you're not sure."

"Never sure of anything with him."

Fallon asked, "Where's your phone?"

"We don't have a phone."

"Not a land line, maybe. Cell phone."

"Yeah, well, whatever."

"Where do you keep it?"

"Purse. On the vanity."

He moved over there, opened the purse with his free hand, rummaged around inside until he found her cell phone. Then he gestured again with the Ruger and they went back into the living room, where he tossed the phone onto an ugly plaid couch.

"Sit down there," he said, "and call Bobby J. And don't try to tell me he doesn't have a cell. I know he does."

"Call him and say what?"

"Tell him to come home right away. Tell him you just got here and there was a break-in while you were out and the house has been trashed."

"That won't get him here. He doesn't give a shit about this place."

"Then tell him something that will get him here."

"Like what? I can't think of anything."

"I can," Fallon said. "You've got a hot new teenage runaway on the hook and he'd better come quick before she wiggles off. You brought her home and she's here waiting."

"He won't believe that. I don't have anything to do with that part of his life. A party once in a while, sure, but that's all."

Now she was lying. "Everybody in Vegas is into one scam or another, and you're no exception. Call him, Candy, and make it sound right."

"What if he doesn't answer?"

"Leave a short message, tell him to call back ASAP. Either way, don't say anything to warn him."

"Or else what?"

"You don't want to find out."

"What're you gonna do to him? Beat him up? Kill him?"

He looked at her without answering.

"What'd he do to you, anyway?"

He didn't answer that, either.

She said, "What about me? What're you gonna do to me?"

"Nothing, if you cooperate."

He watched her think it over. Then, "Fuck it. You know what? I don't really care what you do to him. He treats me like crap most of the time. Maybe he deserves a taste of what it's like."

"Go ahead, make the call."

She made it. Bobby J. didn't answer; the call went to his voice mail. She left the message he'd told her to, brief and terse.

When she broke the connection, he said, "Now call the Golden Horseshoe, tell them you won't be in tonight. Make up an excuse."

"Hey, listen, they don't like us calling in at the last minute. You want me to lose my job?"

"Just keep doing what you're told."

She grumbled some more but she did it. "Now what?"

"Now we wait for Bobby J. to call."

"For how long? It might be hours before he checks his messages. Once he went off someplace and didn't call for three damn days . . ."

"Hours, days, it doesn't matter," Fallon said. "As long as it takes."

Candy was a poor waiter. She fidgeted on the couch, she got up and walked around, she threw dagger glares at him every couple of minutes. Once, after an hour, she unleashed a tirade of four-letter words that he didn't respond to. He sat in the same place with the Ruger on his lap, watching her, the tension in him tamped down under a layer of cold patience. For the most part he kept his mind blank, and when he did think, it wasn't about her or Jablonsky. Casey and Kevin. Timmy. Death Valley and the desert solitude.

Two hours.

The windows were curtained and as dusk settled outside, the room darkened. He told Candy to turn on a couple of lamps. When she'd done that, she stood scowling down at him, her arms folded across her heavy breasts. The robe was still open, showing more freckled white flesh.

"I need a drink," she said. "Steady my nerves."

"It's your house. Help yourself."

"Liquor's out in the kitchen."

"So's the back door."

"Come with me then, for Chrissake—"

Her cell phone rang.

The sudden fluttery ringtone made her jump. She looked at Fallon, did the lip-licking thing again, and flipped it open. Bobby J. The conversation lasted less than a minute. Fallon stood close to her, holding the Ruger where she could see it, to make sure she'd didn't try to warn Jablonsky.

"He's coming," she said.

"Alone?"

"Yeah. Alone."

"Where was he calling from?"

"Golden Horseshoe. Finally checked his goddamn messages when he saw I wasn't there."

Fallon took the phone from her, made sure it was switched off, then slid it into the pocket with the cartridges from the Saturday night special. "Shouldn't take him more than half an hour."

"So what when he gets here? You start shooting up the place?"

"It's not going to be like that. As long as you keep your mouth shut when he comes in."

Twenty-seven minutes had ticked off on Fallon's watch when headlights flashed across the dark front window and he heard the Mustang slide nois-ily into the driveway. He said to Candy, "Stay there and keep still," and got up and moved over at an angle between her and the door.

Hard steps on the porch. The door opened inward, toward where Fallon was standing so that the man coming in didn't see him until he was three paces inside and flinging the door shut behind him. His eyes picked out Candy on the couch, shifted, and when he saw Fallon he froze.

Fallon thumbed the Ruger to full cock. "Guess who, Bobby J.," he said.

FOUR

U P CLOSE, IN A lighted room, Bobby J. was pretty much what Fallon
had expected. Squat and blocky in slacks and a white T-shirt that
showed off his pecs and the fire-breathing dragon tattoo that covered his
right wrist and extended a couple of inches up his hairy forearm. Ice-blue
eyes, empty except for a predatory cunning—the eyes of a man who cared
about no one but himself, who was capable of any act that benefited or pro-
tected Bobby Jablonsky. Flat, hard features. The kind of aggressive, tough-
guy look and manner that attracted women like Candy.

Outwardly he reminded Fallon of a kick-ass drill sergeant he'd known at
Fort Benning, a career soldier who had been in Nam and talked about killing
men as casually and dispassionately as an exterminator talked about killing
bugs. Every grunt who'd encountered him feared his wrath and hated his
guts. The difference between the sergeant and Jablonsky was on the inside.
The sergeant had discipline, moral fiber, the stones and steel it took to lead
men and fight battles. Bobby J. was all hardshell belligerence, powerful only
when he had the upper hand; down deep where it counted, he was a coward.
You could break him if you handled him right. You couldn't have broken the
sergeant with a sledgehammer.

The Ruger didn't seem to scare Jablonsky, but he respected it enough not
to make any stupid moves. He stood flatfooted, hating Fallon with those
empty eyes. Fallon gave it back to him, just as hard and implacable.

"What the fuck you doing in my house?" Growly tough-guy voice to go
with the tough-guy demeanor.

"It's not your house."

Candy said from the couch, "I couldn't help it, Bobby. He just came busting in with that gun—"

"How long's he been here?"

"I don't know, three hours. More."

"He do anything to you?"

"No. Just looked around and made me call you."

Jablonsky said to Fallon, "How'd you find out where I live?"

"It wasn't hard. I know a lot about you."

"Yeah? What do you know?"

"I know about your deal with Court Spicer, for one thing. I know you were down in Laughlin and Bullhead City last night."

"Wrong, man. I ain't been down there in months."

"He said you raped somebody," Candy said. "Is that right? Did you?"

"No. What'd you tell him about me?"

"Nothing. He wanted to know where you were last night, I told him I don't have a clue. Out raping somebody else, for all I know."

"Shut your mouth," Bobby J. said to her, and then to Fallon, "You're not a cop. Who the hell are you? What you want with me?"

"Payback for what you did to Spicer's ex-wife and son—"

"I never done nothing to that kid."

"—and for what you and Clem Vinson were planning to do to me Sunday night."

"How'd you know—" The shape of his expression changed; he rotated the cat's-eye ring on his finger, closed the hand into a fist. "Yeah. That stupid Arbogast."

Fallon let him believe it.

Candy said, "What's this about you and Clem?"

"Didn't I tell you to shut up?"

"Fuck you, Bobby."

"Say that once more and I'll kick your face in."

Fallon said, "You like to beat up on women, don't you? Makes you feel like a big man."

"Yeah, the way you feel with that gun in your hand. Put it down, then we'll find out who's the big man."

"I've got a better idea." Fallon glanced at Candy. "You keep a flashlight in the house?"

". . . Flashlight? Why?"

"Go get it. And don't come back with anything else."

She got up, glared at Bobby J., and disappeared into the kitchen.

Jablonsky said, "You want to run your mouth to me, all right, but don't say nothing more in front of her."

"I don't intend to."

In half a minute Candy was back with a short, stubby flashlight. He motioned for her to come around behind the couch, took the light from her, motioned for her to sit down again. The beam was strong and steady when he switched it on to test it. He shoved it into his empty jacket pocket.

"Okay," he said to Bobby J. "Now we go for a ride."

"What the hell you mean, a ride? Where?"

"You'll find out."

"I'm not going anywhere with you, man."

"Yes, you are. Give me any trouble, I'll blow a hole in your kneecap. You can't even imagine the pain."

"You wouldn't do that. Not with a cannon like that, in this neighborhood."

No, he wouldn't, but Bobby J. didn't know that. "Try me," he said.

Poker player, Jablonsky, but that didn't mean he was good at reading bluffs. And even if he had been, he wouldn't take the risk. He ran his will up against Fallon's for less than a minute before backing down. He shrugged and said sullenly, trying to save face, "You're calling the shots—for now."

Candy said, "What about me?"

"You stay here," Fallon said.

"What, tied up, locked in a closet?"

"Neither one. You could go to one of the neighbors and call the police, but if that was an option you'd've done it when I sent you for the flashlight. So you'll just stay here."

"Why won't I call the cops?"

"Tell her why, Bobby J."

"Don't be stupid," Jablonsky said to the woman. "Do what he says. I'll take care of Slick here."

"Couple of macho jerks," she said contemptuously. She wasn't afraid for herself any longer, or for Bobby J. She didn't even look at him as he went out into the cool night with Fallon behind him.

"We'll take your Mustang. You drive. Keep to the legal speed limit."

"Where the hell we going?"

"Head over to West Charleston."

The Mustang was in good shape. Refurbished interior to match the original upholstery, engine tuned, clutch tight, four-speed transmission in perfect sync. Jablonsky handled it with a kind of fierce, angry pride, slamming through the gears but not popping the clutch to make the tires squeal.

When they reached Charleston, Fallon told him to turn west and keep going. Bobby J. wanted to know how far. He didn't get an answer.

Neither of them had anything to say until they neared the outer rim of the city. From there, you could see distant black cut-out shapes jutting high and ragged across the clear night sky—the Spring Mountains. Between the mountains and the Vegas perimeter was open desert, the Mojave outback.

"What the hell?" Bobby J. said.

"Just keep on toward Red Rock Canyon."

"You can't get in there this time of night—"

"That's not where we're going."

When they'd gone a few miles into the outback, there was almost no traffic. They rolled past thick stands of Joshua trees backdropped by the sheer Spring Mountain walls. There was a three-quarter moon on the rise and in its pale light the misshapen trees had a grotesque, otherworldly aspect.

Bobby J. said, "How much farther, for Chrissake?" For the first time there was an undertone of scare in his voice.

"Not far. There's an old mining road that angles off to the north." Fallon remembered it from one of his hiking trips out here. "Take that when we get to it."

"What for? What're you gonna do?"

"Maybe the same thing you and Clem Vinson were planning at the slot machine repair place."

"You don't know what you're talking about. Wasn't anybody there but me."

"You're a lousy liar, Bobby. I was there, I followed you when you left in Vinson's SUV. That's how I found out where you live."

"Jesus." Then, "We weren't gonna do anything to you. Just talk, that's all. Private talk."

"That's what we're going to have, a private talk."

"Didn't have to come out in the desert for that."

"Sure we did."

"Why?"

Fallon didn't answer that.

After a few seconds Jablonsky said, "Who the hell are you, Slick? What's your connection with the Dunbar woman?"

"What's yours with Court Spicer?"

"Spicer. Listen—"

"There's the road. Make the turn."

It was more of a rutted track than a road, barely discernible, snaking off toward the looming black mountains and the remains of a long-abandoned gold mine. The Mustang jounced and rattled, making the headlights dance eerily over the deformed shapes of the Joshuas and clusters of creosote bushes and crawls of cholla cactus that flanked both sides of the track. Bobby J. said once, "Car's too low-slung for this kind of road. We'll blow a tire, tear up the undercarriage." Fallon said nothing, alternately watching Jablonsky and the terrain, waiting for the right spot.

They'd gone between two and three miles when the track hooked sharply up over a sandhill and down into another dense Joshua thicket. Good a place as any. The Mustang's headlights seemed smothered by the branches and their bayonet-shaped leaves; they weren't likely to be seen by anyone passing on the Red Rock Canyon highway.

"Stop here," he said.

Jablonsky muttered something unintelligible, but he did as he was told. The car settled and the beams held steady on the narrow ruts ahead.

"Shut off the engine but leave the lights on. Then get out and stand in front of the car where I can see you."

"This is bullshit."

"You heard me. Do it."

Bobby J. silenced the engine, but instead of getting out he eased around on the seat, both hands opening and closing around the steering wheel. Fallon could feel the shrewd measuring look, could almost hear the wheels turning inside the man's head.

He was on the verge of a warning when Jablonsky made his move. Hit the light switch, swaddling the Mustang in a blanket of darkness, and lunged sideways, clawing at the Ruger.

Fallon did the opposite of what he'd been expected to do. He moved into the lunge instead of away from it, jabbing his bent and stiffened left arm upward, at the same time bringing the gun in under the groping hand. His elbow caught Bobby J. squarely in the middle of his face; the Ruger's muzzle slammed into his body just below the breastbone. He heard cartilage break mushily, felt a thin spray of blood against the back of his hand. Jablonsky shrieked and jackknifed forward into the wheel, his chin cracking against the horn and unleashing a brief racket.

Fallon said, "Try that again, you're a dead man," and jabbed harder with the gun barrel.

"My nose!" Strangled voice, thick with pain. "You broke my fucking nose!"

"Put the lights back on."

Bobby J. fumbled for the switch. Headlight beams cut through the darkness again, dashboard lights let Fallon see the blocky shape next to him. Jablonsky was still bent forward around the gun, his right hand splayed tight against his face. Blood gleamed black as oil in the dash glow.

"Get out of the car. Now!"

No argument, no hesitation. Bobby J. did some more fumbling, got the door open. He was halfway out when Fallon pulled the Ruger away from his midsection and shoved him, hard, with the other hand. Jablonsky staggered out, lost his balance and slid down on all fours. In less than five seconds, Fallon was out on the passenger side, leaning across the hood with the revolver extended.

But there was no more fight in Bobby J. He kept on kneeling on the hardpan, supporting himself with his left hand, his right once more pressed tight against his fractured nose. The sound of his breathing was loud, ragged, punctuated by little whistling grunts.

"Get up. Walk out on the road and stand in the headlights."

Jablonsky struggled to follow the order. It was ten seconds before he could lift himself upright; his steps were wobbly as he moved into the headlight glare.

"That's far enough. Face the car and stay put."

Watching him, Fallon leaned back into the car long enough to take the keys from the ignition and wipe the blood-spray from his hand on the seatback. Then he moved ahead to stand next to the front bumper. The night was soundless now, that sweet desert stillness; the fast-cooling air smelled of sage, creosote, ancient earth and rock. Above, the sky was powdered with moonlight and flecked with stars bright as crystal. On the track ahead Bobby J. stood swaying, fingering his nose, his face drawn in, tight and blood-smeared, around his shielding hand.

Fallon said, "Take off your clothes."

". . . What?"

"You heard me. Strip. Everything off."

"You're crazy, man. You're fucking nuts."

He extended the Ruger in the radius of light from the headlamps. "You think a busted nose hurts? A shattered kneecap's ten times worse."

Jablonsky lowered his hand; splotches of blood glistened on the tattoo as if it was the dragon that had been wounded. Angrily he ripped off his jacket and shirt, threw them down. Pants next. Boots, socks. Underwear. He stood glaring and whitely naked in the yellow-white cones.

"Kick everything over this way except your undershirt. You can keep that for your nose."

"Goddamn faggot, huh? Like looking at a big hunk of meat?" The words were meant to be cutting and defiant; they came out sounding like a pathetic schoolyard taunt.

"Do what you're told. All right, now back up a few more steps."

"What's the idea?" Jablonsky said, backing.

The idea was simple. An old military tactic that had been used for centuries before Guantánamo and Abu Ghraib. Strip a prisoner naked in front of a fully dressed interrogator, make him feel defenseless and humiliated, and you gain a strong psychological advantage: a naked man doesn't lie easily or well, particularly one with an injury that he'd brought on himself.

Fallon didn't believe in torture on principle, but these were special circumstances. And Bobby J. was a pig.

"That's far enough. Now we'll have our talk."

"Talk? Like this?"

"Why did you kill Court Spicer?"

Jablonsky stopped mopping blood with the undershirt. "Why did I—Jesus Christ! Spicer's *dead*?"

"You know he is."

"Like hell I do. When? What happened?"

"Last night. Shot in his rented house in Bullhead City."

"And you think I did it?"

"Pretty good bet."

"No way! I done a lot of things, but I never shot nobody. I don't even own a gun."

"I'll say it again, Jablonsky: you're a lousy liar. I found the Saturday night special under your mattress."

". . . Yeah, all right, but I never fired it, not one time."

"What about your other piece?"

"I don't have another piece."

"Small caliber, twenty-two or thirty-two."

"No. I never owned one of those."

Fallon said, "We'll see about that. Don't move."

He backed up around the open passenger door, slid into the bucket on one hip. The glove compartment was locked; the ignition key unlocked it. He shined the flashlight inside. Pint bottle of sloe gin. Unopened packet of condoms. Handful of papers that he held up one at a time for brief looks, keeping Bobby J. in sight with his other eye. Registration. Insurance card. Unpaid parking tickets.

No gun. No drugs, either.

Fallon lifted himself out again, shut the door, and backpedaled to the rear. He unlocked the trunk, aimed the flash beam in there. The trunk floor was covered with a rubber mat; nothing on it that could be dried blood, and no signs of recent cleaning. Spare tire. Jack. Toolbox. He opened the box, felt around inside. Just tools—no sidearm. The only other object in the trunk was a gray, rough-weave blanket. He pulled it out, shook it open, ran the light over it. Dirt, but no stains.

He switched off the flash, tossed it into the trunk. Then, leaving the lid up, he went to stand again at the front fender.

Bobby J. said, "I told you I got no other gun."

"That's not all I was looking for."

"What the hell else?"

"Evidence that Casey Dunbar and her son were in the car, alive or dead."

"Oh, man, you really are nuts. I haven't seen her since . . ."

"Since you raped her at the Rest-a-While."

"It wasn't rape. She asked for it. And I never even laid eyes on that kid of hers."

"The boy was in the house when Spicer was shot. He's missing now. So's his mother. Whoever killed Spicer kidnapped one or both of them."

"It wasn't me!"

A thin, raw wind was blowing now, kicking up little whorls of sand that glinted mica-like in the headlights. You could see Bobby J. shiver when the wind gusted, but he didn't wrap his arms around himself. To him, it would have been a sign of weakness. The blood had stopped running out of his nose, but there were streaks of it like Indian warpaint on his cheeks, his bare chest.

"I'm being straight with you," he said, "I swear to God. Let me put my clothes back on, all right? I'm freezing here."

"No. You weren't home last night. Where were you?"

"Losing three bills playing Texas Hold 'Em. Javelina Casino in Henderson, from around five until after midnight."

"People there know you? Players, dealers?"

Bobby J. jumped all over that. "Yeah, sure, they know me. Dealer's name is Ruiz, Hector Ruiz. Ask him, he'll tell you."

"Where'd you go after you quit playing poker?"

"With a woman, to her place. Annie Harris, blackjack dealer at the Javelina." Pain and cold had put a whine in the growly voice. "Ask her, she'll tell you."

Fallon said, "Tell me about you and Spicer. How the two of you hooked up. What kind of deal you had with him."

"He put the word out he needed some new ID. I heard about it, got in touch. I got connections, I know people do that kind of work."

"When was that?"

"Five, six months ago."

"Where'd you deliver the ID to him? Laughlin? His place in Bullhead City?"

"No. Here in Vegas. I never saw him down there. Didn't have no idea where he was living."

"What else you do for him? Help him work his blackmail scam?"

"Blackmail? Christ, I don't know nothing about blackmail. I didn't see him again till ten days ago. He called me up, said he was going to a party at some rich guy's place in Henderson. Said meet him there, he had a proposition for me."

"Beating up and raping his ex-wife."

"No. Knock her around a little, deliver a message to lay off trying to find him. The other thing . . . she asked for it, I told you that—"

"Shut up," Fallon said. "No more lies."

A long way off, a coyote bayed; the sudden sound made Bobby J. twitch and shiver again.

"How much did Spicer pay you?"

"A thousand. He said ask her for another two K, she'd bring it. You want it back? I still got most of it stashed away—"

"He knew he'd been traced to Vegas. How?"

"Private cop she hired asking questions. Some musician he knows told him about it."

"Did he know the private cop? Have any contact with him?"

"Didn't say nothing about that. Just deliver the message, that's all."

"After you delivered it—then what? You see him again?"

"No. Talked on the phone a couple of times."

"After I showed up using his name?"

"Yeah. He thought you must be another private cop."

"Make you a proposition to take care of me too?"

"No. That thing Sunday night . . . my idea. Just a talk, like I said. Find out who you were, convince you to lay off."

"Beat me up. Dump me somewhere. Then hit Spicer up for more money."

"No! I told you—"

Fallon said, "Back up a few more paces."

"Why? What happens now?"

"Back up."

Jablonsky obeyed haltingly. Fallon moved forward into the light, bent to scoop up the pile of clothing and boots.

"You gonna let me get dressed?"

"No."

"Come on, man, I told you everything I know. I got to get to a doctor . . ."

"No."

"Hey, come *on*! I told you everything I know . . ."

Fallon retreated to the trunk, threw the armload inside. Before he slammed the lid, he removed the dirty blanket. He went around to the driver's side, tossed the blanket onto the sandy ground. Then he opened the driver's door.

"Hey," Jablonsky said, "hey, you ain't gonna just leave me here with a busted nose and a lousy blanket? I'll freeze to death out here!"

No, he wouldn't. The blanket and the long walk would keep him warm enough. Once he got to the highway, a police patrol or Good Samaritan would come along and he could make up a story about being robbed and stripped and beaten up and his car stolen at gunpoint.

Fallon got into the Mustang, fired it up. Over the engine roar he heard Bobby J. yell, "Motherfucker! I'll get you for this!"

Like hell he would.

He backed up until he came to a hardpan area at the foot of the sandhill where he could turn around. The last he saw of Bobby J., the last he ever wanted to see of him, Jablonsky had picked up the blanket and was swirling it around himself like a wounded albino bat with dirty gray wings.

FIVE

FRUSTRATION CHEWED ON FALLON again as he drove back into Vegas. Bobby Jablonsky was a liar, a pimp, a rapist, an all-around sleaze-bag, and there wasn't much doubt that he had the capacity for cold-blooded murder under the right circumstances, but he hadn't shot Court Spicer. Or taken Kevin. Or been responsible for Casey's disappearance. He wasn't bright enough to fake his surprise. He hadn't been scared enough for a coward guilty of homicide. And he wouldn't have thrown out all those alibi names so readily if he hadn't been where he claimed he was last night. Another girlfriend might lie for him, but not a Texas Hold 'Em dealer or a roomful of poker players at a Henderson casino.

Fallon retraced Bobby J.'s route back to Sandstone Street, nosed the Mustang to the curb around the corner behind where he'd parked the Jeep. Left it unlocked, with the keyring dangling from the ignition, Candy's cell phone on the seat, and the Saturday night special cartridges strewn on the floor. As he drove away, he had an image of Jablonsky, wrapped in that blanket, hoof-ing it alone out there in the cold desert night. The image gave him no satis-faction. Bad night for Bobby J., but it was a lot less punishment than he deserved.

Well, that could be remedied. Maybe there was nothing Fallon could do about David Rossi's hit-and-run felony, but Jablonsky was a different story. When he found Casey and her son, and he was his own free man again, he'd put an anonymous flea in the ear of the Vegas cops: Bobby J., Max Arbogast, the teenage drug parties at the Rest-a-While. That way, his conscience wouldn't bother him so much and he'd sleep better at night.

By the time he reached his motel, he'd decided something else, too. There were no answers in Vegas. Wherever Casey and the boy were, it wasn't here, any more than it was in Laughlin or Bullhead City.

One other place to look.

And one other possibility for the shooter. It had come to him out in the desert while he was questioning Bobby J.—a name he'd have considered before if he hadn't been so focused on Jablonsky and the Rossis.

The private detective, Sam Ulbrich.

PART V
SAN DIEGO

ONE

FALLON WENT OVER IT and over it on the five-hour, three-hundred-and-fifty-mile drive to San Diego, and Sam Ulbrich was the only way he could make it all fit together. Ulbrich had traced Spicer to Las Vegas; he could have traced him to Laughlin and Bullhead City, too, using his own resources and making his own luck. If his one brush with the state board of licenses was any indication, the man didn't have a lot of scruples. So he might've gone to Spicer's rented house to try a shakedown of his own—blackmail the blackmailer. Only something had gone wrong and Spicer had ended up dead, with the boy as a witness.

Casey might have been another witness, but that explanation still didn't ring true. There was a more likely answer: Ulbrich had contacted her on her cell phone right after the shooting, told her he had her son and offered her a deal, Kevin in exchange for some kind of guarantee of the boy's silence and hers. She'd have jumped at it. Agreed to any terms to get her son back safely.

Best-case scenario, and logical enough as far as it went. But there was a flaw in it. If that kind of deal had been made, she and Kevin should be home by now. And nobody had picked up when Fallon called the Avila Court number again before leaving Vegas.

Near dawn he stopped in Quartzsite, halfway down Highway 95, for gas and a packaged sandwich, and tried her number once more. Nobody picked up this time either.

Where were they, then?

One possibility: part of the deal between Ulbrich and Casey was that she didn't return to San Diego, that she take the boy and disappear the way Spicer had. It didn't satisfy Fallon because it didn't explain why her Toyota was still parked at McCarran International, but he clung to it anyway. The other alternative, that they were both dead, he refused to consider.

San Diego.

Another land-gobbling urban creature, its concrete arteries bloated with morning commuters. Speed up, slow down, stop and go, crawling toward the city's heart—to be pumped out again in eight or nine hours, then pumped back in tomorrow in an endless loop. Early sunlight already beating down on the segmented lines of metal bodies, throwing off laserlike glints and flashes that stabbed the eyes. Highway 95 might have been one of the freeways in L.A. and he might be on his way to work at Unidyne, as on every weekday morning for the past dozen years. One of the faceless multitudes, robbed of his identity for the duration of the ride. No longer free. Engulfed by noise.

Engines. L.A., Vegas, here—all the same. Vast humming, throbbing, roaring man-made turbines composed of millions of interchangeable moving parts. Running in perpetual motion, never still.

This was when he heard them loudest, when he was one of those moving parts. This was when his hunger for escape was the greatest.

Confidential Investigative Services was in the North Park section of San Diego, between University Avenue and the upper corner of Balboa Park. The building, three stories, nondescript, housed a mix of a dozen small professional services—personal injury and family lawyers, certified public accountants, and the like. Ulbrich's office was on the third floor, front. And closed up tight when Fallon arrived there a little after nine. The lettering on the door gave no hours, just the agency's and Ulbrich's names.

The office across the hall housed a firm of CPAs. He tried that door, found it open, and walked in. Behind a desk in the anteroom a middle-aged woman sat making an appointment with somebody on the phone. When she finished, Fallon told her he was looking for Sam Ulbrich and asked what time he opened for business.

"Well, I don't believe he has set hours," the woman said. "Catch as catch can. Have you tried reaching him by phone?"

"Not yet. Would you know if he's been in his office the past couple of days?"

"No, I'm sorry. I haven't seen him, but that doesn't mean he wasn't in."

"Do you have a phone book I can look at?"

She did. There was a small ad for Confidential Investigative Services in the yellow pages, and a white pages listing for Ulbrich, S., on Descanto Street in National City. Fallon wrote down both numbers and the address.

Before he went downstairs, he spoke to people in two other third-floor offices. No one could tell him anything about the detective's business hours, or remembered seeing Ulbrich on Monday or Tuesday.

A call to the detective's home number got him an answering machine. That could mean Ulbrich was in transit. Fallon went to a nearby coffee shop, forced himself to take his time eating a light breakfast—the first food other than the packaged sandwich he'd had in nearly twenty hours. Half an hour later, he was back at the door to Confidential Investigative Services.

Still locked.

He couldn't keep hanging around here, on the chance that Ulbrich would show up. Better try to press it. Back in the lobby he called the Confidential number—another answering machine—and then Ulbrich's home number again. He left brief messages on both machines, giving a made-up name and asking for a callback and an appointment ASAP to discuss a professional matter.

As tired as he was from the long drive, he was too keyed up to sit in one place. He let the Jeep's GPS guide him to National City and Ulbrich's home address, an apartment building just below the San Diego line. Lower middle-class, racially mixed neighborhood, the building a three-story walkup and as nondescript as the one where Ulbrich had his office. So his business couldn't be all that profitable. Scraping by, probably, on domestic and insurance work. The kind of small-timer who'd overcharge a client if he thought he could get away with it, even though he'd been exonerated on the one charge five years ago. Who'd be inclined to cross the line into blackmail if the situation looked ripe enough.

Fallon rang Ulbrich's bell, got nothing for the effort. Two other tenants answered their bells, but neither would talk to him about Ulbrich. On the same block were a small grocery store and a dry-cleaning place. Better cooperation there, but no information. The merchants knew Ulbrich, but not well enough to remember seeing him recently or to describe his habits. Evidently he didn't spend much time in the neighborhood, kept pretty much to himself when he was there.

North Park and the Confidential office again. Running around in zigzag loops, going over and over the same ground the way he had in Vegas when he was hunting Bobby J. But what else could he do?

When he walked into the lobby this time, a fat, tired-looking man in overalls was perched on a tall ladder replacing a burned-out fluorescent ceiling tube. Fallon rode the elevator to the third floor. Ulbrich's office was still closed tight. He rode back down to the lobby, where the overalled man was just coming down off his ladder. Fallon asked him if he worked here regularly. Affirmative; he was the building's maintenance superintendent.

"So then you must know Sam Ulbrich."

"Oh sure, I know Mr. Ulbrich. Been here almost as long as I have."

"Last time you saw him?"

"Couple of days ago."

"Monday?"

The super's face screwed up in thought. "No, it wasn't Monday. Must've been last Friday. That's right, last Friday around noon. He was on his way out to lunch at O'Finn's."

"A place he goes regularly?"

"When he's here. He's away a lot on business. I guess you know Mr. Ulbrich's a private eye. He doesn't like you to call him that, but that's what he—"

"Where is it, this restaurant?"

"Not a restaurant," the super said. "They serve food, but it's a pub, Irish pub. I go there myself sometimes. Great corned beef and cabbage." He glanced at his watch. "Almost noon. Some of that corned beef and cabbage would go good today, now I think of it."

"O'Finn's. Where?"

"Up on University, half a block east."

Fallon found it easily enough. Typical urban Irish pub, with shamrock-and-shillelagh décor inside and out. Long, brass-railed bar, clusters of tables covered by Kelly green cloths, a row of high-backed wooden booths parallel to the bar. Most of the lunch trade hadn't come in yet; the score or so of customers were either grouped at the bar or occupying the booths.

He bellied up to the plank. When the bearded bartender came his way, he said, "You know Sam Ulbrich? Has an office over on Chenango Street, comes in regularly for lunch."

"Sure, I know him."

"Seen him recently?"

"That I have."

"When?"

"Oh, about three seconds ago."

". . . What?"

The bartender laughed. "Right behind you. Third booth from the front."

TWO

FALLON TURNED TO PEER across the room. He hadn't expected anything walking over here, but he'd finally caught a piece of luck. He hesitated, watching the man in the booth hoist a pint of Guinness. Brace him here and now? Or wait until he was finished and then follow him and brace him when he was somewhere by himself? Either way, he would have to do it without the Ruger for leverage. The sidearm was still locked inside the Jeep.

He went to the booth, walking slow, getting a read on Ulbrich on the way. Midfifties, heavy-set, craggy features, close-cropped iron-gray hair. Wearing a short-sleeved blue shirt, no tie, in deference to the warm weather. There was a sports jacket folded neatly on the seat beside him. If he was armed, it was probably a hideout piece and he'd have to be crazy to flash it in here.

"Sam Ulbrich?"

Ulbrich looked up, cocked his head to one side when he didn't recognize Fallon. "That's me."

"My name's Fallon." No reaction. "I'd like to talk to you."

"Business?"

"That's right."

"Well, I've just ordered lunch. First food I've had a chance at all day—I've been on a job in Lemon Grove since seven. Join me and we can talk while we eat. Or if you'd rather wait until afterward, my office isn't far . . ."

"Here'll do."

"Corned beef's the house specialty," Ulbrich said. "Lamb stew with black pudding's good, too, if you like black pudding."

"I'm not hungry."

"Guinness? Ale?"

"Just talk."

Ulbrich shrugged, lifted his glass again as Fallon sat down opposite. On his right forearm was a faded tattoo of the Marine Corps EGA, a spread-winged American eagle holding in its beak an unfurled banner with the words *Semper Fi* emblazoned on it. Ulbrich saw him looking at it, said, "Four and out in the early seventies. You ever in the military?"

"Army. MPs. Four years."

"MPs, huh? I went into police work when I got out. San Diego force for fifteen years."

Fallon said nothing.

"See any action on your tour?"

"No."

"Me, neither. Came close, though. My company was in Saigon, just sent over from the Philippines, when the war ended." Ulbrich drank again. "I was lucky. Sounds like we both were."

Fallon was silent again.

"So. What can I do for you, Mr. Fallon?"

"You can tell me where to find Casey Dunbar and her son."

Like tossing a dud grenade. A raised eyebrow was Ulbrich's only reaction. His gaze remained steady on Fallon's eyes, its only expression one of curiosity.

"What's your interest in the Dunbars?"

"I'm a friend of Casey."

"Is that right? Then you ought to know where to find her."

"She's missing. She's been missing since Monday night."

"Is that right?" Ulbrich said again. "Well, I'm sorry to hear it. But why come to me?"

"You found her ex-husband for her."

"I wish that was true, but it isn't. I traced Court Spicer to Vegas, but that was as far as I got. I might've been able to find him eventually if I'd stayed on the case, but she couldn't afford to keep paying the bills—"

"Laughlin," Fallon said. "Bullhead City."

"I don't get you."

"Rented house. Sixty Desert Rose Lane."

"Is that supposed to mean something to me?"

Another dud. Fallon felt uncertainty moving in on him again. He'd convinced himself Ulbrich was his man, yet the responses he was getting didn't support it. Not a whisper of guilt.

Ulbrich said, "So Mrs. Dunbar is missing. Monday night, you said? Where? What circumstances?"

Fallon said carefully, "The last I saw of her was in Laughlin."

"Laughlin. Why go there?"

"Hunting for Court Spicer."

"What made you think that's where he was?"

"Lucky piece of information."

"Luck's the name of the game. Find him?"

That put Fallon up against the line again. Tell Ulbrich that Spicer was dead, murdered, see what kind of reaction that bought him? No. The situation here was different than it had been with the Rossis and Bobby J. He'd be leaving himself wide open if Ulbrich wasn't involved. He didn't know the man, how law-abiding he actually was. Ex-cop, licensed private investigator . . . he might take that kind of knowledge straight to the Laughlin authorities.

He said, "No. Casey Dunbar disappeared before we could."

"Two of you hunting her ex together," Ulbrich said musingly. "You're not in the investigation business yourself, are you?"

"No. I told you, she's a friend."

"She didn't mention your name when she hired me."

"I haven't known her that long. How we got involved is a long story. And not relevant right now."

"So what it amounts to, you've been playing detective."

"If you want to put it that way. Four years MP duty, dozen years security work for a company in L.A. I'm not exactly an amateur."

A waiter appeared bearing a steaming plate of corned beef and cabbage, set it down in front of Ulbrich. "Another Guinness," Ulbrich said to him. Then, to Fallon, "Sure you don't want anything?"

Fallon leaned back away from the mingled aromas of the food. They made the eggs he'd had earlier churn in his stomach.

Ulbrich fell to with gusto. Between bites, he said, "You still haven't told me how it happened. Mrs. Dunbar's disappearance."

"She was at the motel where we were staying. I went out to see if I could track down Spicer and when I got back she was gone. No note, nothing—just gone. I haven't heard a word from her since."

"So you've been hunting her for two days."

"That's right."

"What about Spicer? He kidnapped his son, he's capable of snatching his ex-wife too. You must know there's no love lost between them."

"I know, but Spicer's not responsible."

"No? How do you know?"

"Reasons I don't want to go into."

"Suit yourself. If not Spicer, who else? Somebody he knew in Vegas?"

"That's what I thought at first. And that's where I went from Laughlin."

"And you didn't find out anything and now you're here talking to me. Looking for leads, or have you got some screwy idea I'm mixed up in it?"

"Are you?"

"Hell, no." Ulbrich didn't sound any more offended than he did guilty. Cabbage juice drooled from one corner of his mouth; he licked off some of it, wiped the rest away with his napkin. "What possible reason could I have for going to Laughlin, making a former client disappear?"

"I can think of one, if you did locate Spicer and found out about his sideline."

"What sideline would that be?"

"Blackmail."

The eyebrow went up again. "Blackmail. Well, well."

"You don't sound surprised."

"I've been around too long to be surprised by much of anything. So? Why would this blackmail angle interest me?"

"You could've tried to cut yourself in. Or to put the bite on him to keep quiet."

Ulbrich thought that was funny. He laughed, nearly choked on the hunk of corned beef he'd stuffed into his mouth, coughed, swallowed the rest of his beer, coughed some more. "Man," he said when the fit had passed, "you've got some imagination. Either that, or you're so desperate you're grabbing at any straw that blows by in the wind."

"Seems plausible to me."

"Not if you know Sam Ulbrich, it isn't. I've been in one kind of law enforcement or another for nearly thirty years, Fallon. Spotless record. I'd never do anything to jeopardize it."

"What about the time you were brought up before the state board of licenses?"

Ulbrich sobered. "You know about that? Yeah, well," he said darkly, "that was a bogus charge made by a client who was pissed that I couldn't get the kind of evidence he was looking for on a business partner. The judge cleared me, you understand? Completely cleared me."

"Okay, so you didn't know Spicer was a blackmailer. Didn't find out anything along those lines when you were investigating him."

"That's right. And if I had, I wouldn't tell you what it was."

"But you'd have told Casey Dunbar."

"Full disclosure to my clients, always. And nobody else without their permission."

Fallon said, "Where were you Monday night?"

"Still not convinced, huh?"

"So convince me."

"Why the hell should I? I ought to push your face in."

"Welcome to try."

Their eyes locked and held. During the staredown, the waiter returned with the fresh Guinness and that broke it up. A slow, sardonic grin turned up the corners of Ulbrich's mouth. He shrugged, picked up his fork.

"Hell," he said, eating, "I'm not trying to be a hard-ass here. Mrs. Dunbar is missing, you're a friend of hers, you've got a right to be worried. I'd be worried, too, in your shoes."

"You haven't answered my question about Monday night."

"I was right here in San Diego. Imperial Beach, actually."

"You don't live in Imperial Beach."

"That's right, I don't. But my daughter does. With her husband and her two kids. One Monday a month I go out there, have dinner with them, and she tells me all about what her mother's doing these days and I try not to puke while she's doing it. That's where I was last Monday night. You don't believe it, I'll give you my daughter's phone number."

Fallon slumped against the booth back. Wrong again. Sam Ulbrich wasn't any guiltier than David Rossi or Sharon Rossi or Bobby J.

"Truth hurts sometimes," Ulbrich said philosophically. "So where do you go from here, Fallon?"

"I don't know. I don't know where to go or what the hell to think. I just keep stumbling into dead ends."

"Maybe you need some help."

"Maybe I do."

"Professional help. My kind."

Fallon considered it, but only briefly. Even with better resources, what could Ulbrich do that he hadn't already done or couldn't do himself? Something in the long run, maybe, but he needed answers *now*. Besides, it would mean telling him the whole story. All confiding in Ulbrich would accomplish was to put himself into greater jeopardy.

"I don't think so," he said.

"If it's because you're low on money, we can work something out."

"Money's not an issue. I've got to see this through on my own."

Fallon slid out of the booth, started to turn away.

Ulbrich said, "Wait a minute." And when Fallon leaned down, "I don't know that this'll help you much, but you can have it for what it's worth. I had the feeling Casey Dunbar was holding something back when she hired me. Hiding something, maybe."

"Such as what?"

"I don't know. Just an impression I got when we were talking about Spicer and the kid. I can read people pretty well—one of the reasons I'm good at what I do."

"Lying to you?"

"Not exactly. Just not giving me the whole story, leaving out details that I should've been told. You didn't get the same feeling from her?"

"No," Fallon admitted, "I didn't."

"Probably because you wanted to believe her. That's the difference between the personal and professional perspective." Ulbrich lifted his fresh Guinness. "Luck."

"Thanks. I'll need it."

THREE

NOW HE HAD SOMETHING else to think about. Had Casey kept something important from Ulbrich, something that might have a bearing on Spicer's death and her and Kevin's disappearance? If so, then it was likely she'd withheld the same information from him too. Her account of her life and troubles with Spicer had seemed straightforward enough, and nothing he'd found out so far had contradicted it. But he didn't really know her. And as Ulbrich had said, he'd wanted to believe her.

Where do you go from here, Fallon?

Good question, and it kept echoing inside his head as he walked back to where he'd parked the Jeep. No theories left that fit the facts as he knew them. No clear-cut course of action. Options, sure, but Ulbrich had had a phrase that fit them, too, all of them: grabbing at straws blowing by in the wind.

All right. The only thing he could do was to keep grabbing.

Avila Court ran parallel to Adams Avenue, not far from San Diego State University—a ten-minute drive from Ulbrich's office building. Number 716 was an old-fashioned, Spanish-style bungalow court, the kind that had proliferated in southern California in the '30s and '40s but that you didn't see much of anymore. There were eight stucco units in this one, each facing a central courtyard and separated from their nearest neighbors by grass strips and wooden fences.

The courtyard was empty when Fallon walked in. Casey's bungalow was the second in from the street on the left, its stucco front wall age-pocked and in need of a fresh coat of whitewash. Some kind of flowering shrub grew tall in a planter box next to the front door, giving off a cloyingly sweet scent.

A stuffed-full mailbox told him he wouldn't get an answer when he rang the bell. He rang it anyway, three times. Then he reached down to test the knob—another futile gesture.

Salsa music, not too loud, filtered out of one of the bungalows across the way. Its facing window wore a set of closed Venetian blinds, as did the windows on all of the other units except for one at the far end. The angle of the sun let him see through the glass to the room inside that one. Furniture shapes, but nobody moving around.

Casually, as if he belonged there, he took the accumulation of mail out of the box and shuffled through it. Catalogues, two bills, a handful of junk mail. No letters or postcards.

Between Casey's bungalow and the neighbor on the right were a pair of gated areaways separated by a fence, where garbage cans and odds and ends could be stored. Still carrying the mail, Fallon moved over there and lifted the latch. The gate opened inward; he stepped through, shut it again behind him. Two bicycles, one a small boy's, and a pair of garbage cans all but filled the narrow space. The wooden fence was seven feet tall, weathered but in decent repair, built to provide privacy because the bungalows were set so close together.

One window, small and frosted, overlooked the areaway. Bathroom window. On the way to it, he dropped the mail onto one of the cans. When he pushed upward on the frame, it gave an inch or so before binding up. Casey wasn't one of the people who left their bathroom windows unlocked.

Not that it mattered. From the way the sash had moved, he knew it was locked with a simple lever arrangement hooked into a plate in the sill. The largest of the blades in his Swiss Army knife slid easily into the crack. He maneuvered the blade against the lever, wiggled and prodded until it released from the plate. With his left hand he held it balanced on the blade while he pushed the sash up with his right.

It made a creaking noise, loud enough in his ears to freeze him for a few seconds. Closing the knife, he sidled over to the gate. There was a thin gap between two of the boards, wide enough for a view of the courtyard. Still no-body around. He stayed there for a couple of minutes, watching and listen-ing. No one came out of the other bungalows or into the court from the street.

Back to the window. Illegal trespass: one more risk, one more felony added to those he'd already committed—and the hell with worrying about it. He hoisted himself into the opening, ducked his head under the sash, corkscrewed his body until he had one leg and then the other inside.

The bathroom was just large enough for a stall shower, sink, toilet. The toilet was positioned directly below the window, its seat lowered and hid-den inside a furry pink cover. He stepped down onto the linoleum floor, then out into a short hallway.

Two small bedrooms, a kitchen, a dining alcove, a living area with a gas-log fireplace—all the rooms small, almost cramped, and smelling faintly of dust and the mustiness of places closed up for more than a few days. The bungalow had come furnished—the bland sparseness of the pieces told him that—and Casey hadn't made much of an effort to personalize it. But she kept a neat house. Everything in its place, the kitchen sink and counters scrubbed clean, the beds made, the books and other kid things in Kevin's room put away.

Fallon started in the living room, with no idea of what he was looking for. Something, anything—new information, a fresh lead, another straw.

In one corner was a secretary desk, a Dell PC and monitor perched on it. He turned the computer on, booted it up. Casey hadn't installed a pass-word; he was able to open her mailbox and document files. All of the E-mails she'd received during the past week were spam. And all that was stored on the hard drive were a tax file listing income and expenses, another file of PG&E online receipts, and a handful of video games. The Web sites she'd bookmarked told him nothing, either. Health sites dealing with asthma and women's issues, YouTube, eBay, kid-related sites.

He made himself take his time going through the desk drawers and pi-geonholes, putting whatever he looked at back where he'd found it. The usual paperwork: bills, receipts. A Book-of-the-Month Club flyer, a brochure from a youth camp. In one of the drawers was her checkbook, and a filled transac-tion register; the combined entries went back nearly six months. Rent, water and garbage, MasterCard, doctor, dentist, a day-care outfit that had probably looked after Kevin when he wasn't in school and she was working. None of the checks had been written to private individuals.

He scanned through the deposits. On Friday of every week, she banked the salary and commissions she earned from Vernon Young Realty, noted as such in the register—all modest sums. But there were other deposits as well, regularly posted at the beginning of each month, each in the amount of $1,000. The source of that money wasn't noted. He booted up the computer again, checked the tax file. No record of the monthly $1,000. So where did it come from and why wasn't she listing it as income?

There was nothing else in the desk. Or in the rest of the living room; he opened every drawer, even lifted the cushions on the couch and two chairs and examined the backs of the pictures on the walls. The kitchen next. Drawers and cabinets, the refrigerator and its freezer compartment—nothing. He went from there into Casey's bedroom.

The first thing that drew his attention was a silver-framed 8×10 photograph on the nightstand. Professionally done head-and shoulders color portrait of Kevin, his pale hair neatly brushed, his mouth shaped into a shy smile. In this photo you could see that his eyes were light brown, with long, fine lashes. Fallon felt his chest constrict. The boy didn't look anything like Timmy, really. But the longer he looked at Kevin's likeness, the more it seemed to morph into Timmy's.

A dog-eared paperback novel, a package of tissues, a tube of hand cream, and a pair of nail clippers were the only contents of the nightstand drawer. He turned to the mirrored dresser. On top was a teakwood jewelry box that contained a tray of earrings, two bracelets, a necklace, and a brooch, none of the pieces expensive. The dresser drawers held nothing but lingerie and folded shirts and T-shirts.

The closet. Dresses, pantsuits, blouses, slacks, jackets, and a pair of raincoats on hangers; a rack of shoes, an umbrella on the floor; some boxes on the shelf above. All the clothing pockets were empty. He took the boxes down one by one. Some kind of fancy gown in the first, baby clothes in the second. The third contained mementoes, most relating to Kevin—a gold-plated baby spoon, a wallet of baby photos, a lock of fine blond hair. None of the other items meant anything to him, except for a woman's plain gold wedding band without an inscription. He wondered fleetingly why she'd kept it. Not for sentimental reasons, not the way she felt about Court Spicer.

In the bathroom he scanned the contents of the medicine cabinet. The usual over-the-counter medicines and first-aid items, a prescription vial of Ambien, a packet of birth-control pills, an asthma inhaler.

Kevin's bedroom. Fantasy books, a Nintendo Game Boy, a stuffed tiger with a torn ear, a poster illustration from one of the Harry Potter novels. The boy's clothing neatly put away in his dresser and closet. Everything in place, awaiting his return.

Fallon went out of there, hesitated, then on impulse stepped into Casey's bedroom again. He stood sweating in the stuffy air, looking around. He wasn't sure why—just a vague feeling that he'd missed something the first time. Under the bed? He dropped to all fours, lifted the bedskirt to peer beneath. The only things on the carpet were a pair of skeletal dust mice.

When he straightened, his gaze was on the bureau—on the teakwood jewelry box. Its size registered on him for the first time: twelve inches wide, eight or nine inches deep. He opened the lid again. The tray with the earrings and other pieces was only a couple of inches deep, which meant another six inches or so of space. It took a little effort to lift the tray out; there was a fingertip catch that you couldn't see unless you put an eye down close to it. And underneath—

A ribbon-tied sheaf of handwritten notes, a wallet-sized photo album, two small jewelry cases. Casey's secret stash, hidden away in the one place where a small boy was least likely to stumble across them.

Fallon opened the cases first, both of which bore Tiffany's labels. Their velvet-lined innards were empty, the expensive jewelry they'd contained hocked or sold to finance Sam Ulbrich's investigation. Presents from Spicer, bought with the blackmail money from David Rossi. That was what he thought until he read through the bundled notes, looked at the photos.

Those told a different story. The true story about the source of the jewelry, and a lot of other things too.

They told him what she'd withheld from Ulbrich and from him—some of it, anyway. Deliberate lies of omission that had led him in all the wrong directions and jeopardized his freedom.

They told him who might be responsible for Spicer's death.

They told him the probable reason for her and Kevin's disappearance, and how he could go about finding them now.

The notes were all brief, written in a precise, backslanted male hand, some containing promises and sexual innuendo. Only a few were dated; the earliest was October 2000. All were signed with a single initial. The color snapshots were of a lean, handsome man in his forties, of Casey, of the two of them together. Just them, nobody else. Several had been taken around a garden swimming pool with rows of palm trees in the background; in one of those, she'd struck a provocative pose wearing only a pair of bikini swim pants. Fallon took that one out of its glassine envelope. Written in purple ink on the back, in a different hand from the letters—Casey's hand—was "V. and me, Indio, 7/03."

V. The same initial that was on the notes.

V for Vernon. Vernon Young.

She'd been having an ongoing affair with her boss that dated back a long time before her divorce from Court Spicer.

FOUR

VERNON YOUNG REALTY WAS a successful operation, housed in its own stone-and-glass building in an upscale neighborhood near Mission Bay. Eight desks arranged behind a gated counter laden with brochures, flyers, and business cards. Five of the desks were staffed when Fallon walked in, the sales reps, three men and two women, all busy on phones and computers. None of the men was the lean, handsome type in Casey's photo collection.

Fallon said to the receptionist, a young woman with red hair, blue eyes, and a white smile, "I'd like to see Vernon Young."

"Oh, I'm sorry, Mr. Young is out of the office today."

"Hasn't been in all week, has he?"

"No, he hasn't. He's away on a personal matter."

"Where can I reach him? It's important."

"I'm afraid you can't. He's not available."

"Not even by phone?"

"Not at all. If it has to do with a property, perhaps one of our agents can—"

"I need to speak to Mr. Young personally. I left a message for him yesterday, but he didn't get back to me. Has he called in for his messages?"

"No. No, he hasn't. I'm sure he'll be in touch soon, Mr.—?"

"Jablonsky. When do you expect him back in the office?"

"I really don't know. Perhaps tomorrow or Friday. Would you care to leave another message?"

"No. I don't suppose you've heard from Casey Dunbar, either?"

"Why, no. Ms. Dunbar has been on vacation the past week."

Vacation. Sure.

Like the one he'd been on since last Friday.

The woman who answered the phone at the Young home sounded middle-aged, tired, and not overly bright. "Mr. Young's not here. Neither is the missus, but she'll be back pretty soon."

"Who am I talking to?"

"Mrs. Reilly. I'm the cleaning woman."

"Does Mrs. Young know where her husband can be reached, Mrs. Reilly? It's important that I talk to him. I stopped by his office, but they said they don't know where he is."

"I'm sure I don't know either. You'll have to ask the missus."

"How soon will she be back?"

"She said around three. She's at the hairdresser's."

Three o'clock. Close on two-thirty now. Another thirty or forty minutes of downtime.

He said, "I'll come by around three, then. What's the address there?"

"The address?"

"I've only been to the house once, two years ago, and I don't remember the street or number."

"Well . . ."

"It's best if I see Mrs. Young in person. It could mean a big sale for her husband's company."

"It could?" the woman said, but not as if she cared. "Well, I guess it's okay then. One two five five nine Wildwood, San Pasqual Valley. You know, where they had them bad fires last year."

Fallon remembered "them bad fires." They'd been all over the media a year ago this month. Four of them in San Diego County, the two worst in Poway south of Escondido and San Pasqual Valley in the northeast corner of the city. Over 400,000 acres burned, more than a thousand homes destroyed, hundreds of thousands of people evacuated into Qualcomm Stadium and other shelters. The scars were visible in the hills and canyons above the valley, irregular blackened swaths and patches where houses had once stood. New construction flourished in the area; he saw more than a dozen sites on his way up winding Wildwood Road.

He'd never quite understood the willingness of people to rebuild in the same area where a natural disaster had struck. Maybe they thought it couldn't happen again. But this was wildfire country. The homes and the vegetation would grow thick again, the canyons would clog with dry brush, and all it would take to set it off again was another bolt of lightning or incident of human carelessness. One more reason why he preferred the desert. It had its natural dangers, sure, but if you knew what you were doing, you had some control over the risks they presented. In the remote, expensive firetraps in locations like this, you had little or none.

The Youngs had been lucky: the section of Wildwood Road where they lived had escaped devastation. No scars, no new construction visible in the immediate area. The homes and outbuildings all stood on large parcels, built onto the hillsides and atop canyon walls, with stilt-supported decks overlooking the agricultural preserve spread across the valley floor below. Million-dollar properties, minimum. Vernon Young had done all right for himself in the real-estate business.

Fallon's timing couldn't have been better. His watch showed a few minutes past three when the Jeep's GPS guided him to a stop in front of 12559 Wildwood—a redwood-and-glass structure that was all juts and odd angles, as if the architect who'd designed it had been drunk or stoned. The car that had been following him for the last mile or so, a silver-gray BMW, rolled past and turned into the Youngs' driveway. He moved fast enough to intercept the woman who emerged before she could cover the distance between her car and the front door.

"Mrs. Young?"

She stopped and turned, shading her eyes against the lowering sun. "Lucia Tibbets. Yes?"

"You are Vernon Young's wife?"

"I prefer to use my maiden name. What is it you want?"

"Your husband. I'm trying to locate him."

"Yes?"

"Regarding a valuable property in Escondido. The people at his office said he hasn't been in all week."

"And they sent you here?"

"No. My idea. I thought you'd know where I can reach him."

"Well, you were wrong. I haven't seen or talked to my husband since Sunday night."

She started toward the house. Again Fallon moved quickly to block her way. Her body stiffened; irritation showed in eyes that were a peculiar pale gray, almost white in the sun. He took her to be in her late forties, with dyed chocolate-brown hair and the too-smooth features of women who have been repeatedly nipped and tucked and Botoxed. There was a brittleness about her, a brittleness in her voice, that gave him the feeling she kept herself tightly wrapped.

"I really do need to talk to Mr. Young right away," he said. "It could mean a substantial commission—"

"I have nothing to do with my husband's business dealings." Her tone said the choice was his, not hers.

"If you could just give me some idea of where he might be . . ."

One shoulder lifted in a faint shrug. "He comes and goes when and where he pleases. As do I."

So it was that kind of marriage. Fallon wondered if she knew Young had a mistress. Probably. Knew it and didn't care much, if at all, just so long as he paid the bills.

"Please, Mrs. Tibbets. There must be—"

"Ms. I don't like the word missus."

"There must be some place he goes when he wants to get away by himself."

"My husband doesn't go anywhere by himself."

"For privacy, then. Do you have a second home?"

"Oh yes, we have a second home," she said, and the words came out sounding bitter. "That ranch of his."

"Ranch?"

"He bought it fifteen years ago." Over her objection, her tone implied. Sore subject with her. She was the type who'd prefer a beach cottage or mountain hideaway to a ranch. "He worked on one when he was a boy, as

if that's sufficient reason for buying one. At least it pays for itself. He had
the good sense to lease the date groves."

"You said . . . date groves?"

"That's right. Dates. The nasty sweet fruit."

"Where is this ranch?"

"In the desert, of course. Near Indio."

Indio. The snapshot in Casey's stash: "V. and me, Indio, 7/03."

"I'd appreciate it if you'd let me have the address."

"I don't remember the address. I haven't been there in a dozen years.
When I go to the desert, I go to Palm Springs."

"Could you look it up for me?"

"No, I don't think so. When he goes there, he doesn't like to be disturbed."

"Not even for a real estate deal that involves a lot of money?"

"Not for any reason. Why don't you talk to someone in his office? All of
his people are perfectly competent."

"I'd rather deal directly with—"

He broke off because he was talking to her back. She was already on her
way to the house in long, stiff strides, her hips barely moving inside her white
dress as if they, too, had been tightly nipped and tucked.

She must really hate him, he thought. The kind of hate that happens in
some marriages when people stay together for the wrong reasons. The kind
of hate he was glad Geena had never come to feel for him, or he for her.

The nearest Internet café was in a shopping center a few miles away. It
might have been quicker to call Will Rodriguez and ask him to run a property search, but Fallon had bothered him enough as it was. It wouldn't take
him too long to do the job himself. Property searches are simple enough because the information is readily available, no fees required.

Indio was in Riverside County, in the desert twenty-some miles east of
Palm Springs, but it seemed likely the tax bills for Young's date ranch would
be sent to his primary address. So Fallon did a search of the San Diego
County property records, typing Young's name and the Wildwood Road address into the rented computer.

Right. The ranch's address was 5900 San Ignacio Road, Indio.

PART VI

INDIO

ONE

THE DISTANCE FROM San Diego to Indio was better than a hundred and sixty miles, a straight-through drive that should have taken no more than two and a half hours. It took Fallon three because he got hung up, as he had coming in, in the damn stop-and-go commute traffic. He was wired up tight, gritty eyed and functioning on adrenaline and a simmering anger, by the time the Jeep's GPS took him onto San Ignacio Road.

It was some miles outside of town, in the part of the Coachella Valley that was still primarily agricultural. Indio had once been surrounded by date-palm groves that produced a large percentage of the country's date crop, but residential and recreational development had gobbled up all but sections on the south and southeast. More desert land forever lost. One day, sure as hell, there wouldn't be any more of the Old World agricultural staple that had once been the region's lifeblood. Just as there weren't any more orange groves in the San Fernando Valley.

Now, though, geometrical rows of date palms still dominated sections of the sandy desert soil, their crowns swaying in a warm evening breeze. He passed several small ranches, then a Spanish adobe ranch store that looked as if it might be a century old, its illuminated sign claiming it was the home of the finest Medjool dates in the Coachella Valley. Darkness had settled when he reached the access lane marked with the number 5900.

The lane was paved, wide near the entrance, then narrowing somewhat as it led in among the close-packed palms. A shallow drainage culvert ran along the left-hand side. Once Fallon made the turn, he could make out a whitish glow beyond where the lane jogged to the left. Lights from the ranch buildings, he thought. But the guess was wrong.

When he cleared the jog, he was looking at a pair of headlights ahead on his left, a high-beam glare that illuminated the trees in the rows nearest the lane.

Automatically he slowed, eased over to the right. But the other car wasn't moving; it had been drawn up at the edge of the lane where the culvert was. And somebody was in the grove over there—somebody using a not-very-powerful flashlight in erratic, bobbing sweeps that created weird light-and-shadow effects among the tall, straight palm trunks.

The sidespill from the Jeep's headlamps picked out movement in the grove to Fallon's right—just a brief, sliding-past impression of a darting shape. A few seconds later, as he neared the parked car, he could see that its right front wheel was on the edge of the culvert, that the driver's door stood wide open.

He swung the wheel, slewed the Jeep to a stop close to the car's front bumper. He yanked the keys out of the ignition, unlocked the storage compartment. The Ruger was in there; so was his six-cell flashlight. He hesitated over the weapon, left it where it was, slammed the compartment shut, and flicked on the torch as he jumped out.

Above the lane you could see the starlit sky, but the crouching masses of palm crowns created a solid ceiling; in among the trees, except on the side where the flashlight continued to move in restless arcs, it was pitch-black. A faint breeze rustled and rattled in the fronds, carried the sound of a voice raised high and shrill—a woman's voice, calling something he couldn't quite make out.

The other car was a BMW, silver-gray, a twin to the one Vernon Young's wife drove. Fallon ran around to the open driver's door, threw light inside front and back. Empty. The keys still dangled from the ignition. On impulse he reached in for them, shoved them into his pocket.

The woman was still calling, louder, the shift and sway of the flash beam coming nearer. Now he could make out what she was shouting.

"Kevin! Where are you? *Kevin!*"

Casey's voice.

He aimed his flash, more powerful than hers, toward the sound. The nearby palm boles and the sandy ground around and between them leaped into stark relief. A few seconds later she appeared, running and stumbling in his direction, still crying the boy's name in a voice that throbbed with the accents of terror.

She saw him, but at first only as an indistinguishable shape behind the six-cell. Now she was saying, as if to a stranger, "Help me, please . . . my son . . ." Then her light shifted, came up to wash over and then steady on him. He lowered his so she could see him clearly.

She staggered to a halt; the sharp intake of her breath was audible in the stillness. "Oh my God! Rick! Where'd you come from, how did you—"

"Never mind that now. What's happened?"

She stood panting, poised as if to turn and run. He fixed her with the six-cell again. Her face was white, her eyes like black holes thumb-punched in powdered dough. "Kevin," she said then. "He . . . ran away. He's out here somewhere, hiding . . ."

"Why? Why did he run away?"

Mutely she rolled her head from side to side.

"You're sure he's out here?"

"Yes! I saw him, that's why I got out of the car. Oh God, Rick, help me find him! Please!"

Fallon pivoted away from her, ran across to the edge of the grove on the opposite side and back down the road toward where he'd seen the darting shape. Behind him he heard Casey shout, "Not over there, he's on this side . . ." Then the only sounds were the cry of a nightbird, the thin rasp of his breathing.

After fifty yards or so, he cut in to one of the narrow paths between the palms. He'd had the light aimed low as he ran; now he raised it and swung it in wide, sweeping arcs. Trunks, broken fronds, irrigation troughs, a stack of packing boxes burst into sharp relief, vanished again. He tried to make as little noise as possible, didn't call out Kevin's name. If the boy wasn't responding to his mother's voice, he'd be even more frightened by a stranger's.

Twice Fallon paused to listen. Faintly he could hear Casey's frantic voice shouting again, somewhere back near where the Jeep and BMW were. The second time he stopped, he thought he heard a scrabbling sound off to his left. He jabbed the light in that direction, followed it before changing direction again. Not Kevin. A night creature of some kind.

It might have taken a long time to find the boy, if he'd been able to find him at all, if it hadn't been for a panic reaction when Fallon passed close to where he was hiding. The six-cell's white shaft roved past just above his head, flushed him and set him running again down the next row. Fallon veered over there, heard him but didn't see him at first in the thick darkness. Then the light picked him out—running blind, looking back over his shoulder.

The ground here had an obstacle: a long date-picker's ladder, wide at the bottom and almost pointed at the top, had been propped sideways against one of the palm trunks. Kevin didn't see it in time to avoid it. There was a clatter, a yowl of pain, and the boy sprawled headlong.

Fallon was there in five seconds. By then, Kevin was trying to crawl behind one of the palms. He'd hurt himself in the collision with the ladder: dragging and clutching at his left leg, the small face grimacing with pain. He quit crawling when the flash beam pinned him, squinted up into the glare with eyes that gleamed black with fear.

"Leave me alone!" Thin, gasping. "Leave me alone!"

Fallon moved the light out of his face, dropped to one knee beside him. "It's all right, Timmy. I'm not—"

"My name's not Timmy!"

He drew back, realizing what he'd said. Timmy. Jesus, what was the matter with him? It must have been that first clear look at the boy, the strained white face and terrified stare, the lank, light-colored hair plastered wetly to his forehead . . . for just an instant it had been like seeing his son alive again.

"I'm sorry, Kevin. I'm sorry."

The boy cringed away from him, his chest heaving, his breath wheezing and rattling asthmatically.

"It's all right, you don't have to be afraid. I'm not going to hurt you. Lie still, take shallow breaths—"

Kevin sat up instead, tried to propel himself backward with both hands. Fallon stopped him by catching hold of the waistband of his Levi's.

"No, lie still," he said again, and this time the boy obeyed him. "That's it. Shallow breaths now. You have your inhaler?"

". . . Pocket."

Pants pocket. Fallon felt the outline of it, fished it out, watched as Kevin sucked in three deep inhalations. The boy's eyes were still saucer-wide. "Who are you?" he said when the asthma medicine had opened up the breathing passages in his lungs. "I don't know you."

"My name's Rick. I'm a friend of your mom's—"

"No! I won't go back there, I won't!"

"Easy, easy. Where'd you hurt yourself?"

". . . My ankle. I twisted it."

"Let me see how bad."

Fallon screwed the six-cell into the sand. When he ran his fingers gently over the injured ankle, the boy whimpered and cringed again but didn't try to pull away. Nothing broken. Just a strain.

Fallon said, "Let's get you up," and put his hands under Kevin's arms and lifted him without much struggle. It was like lifting a child-sized manikin— the kid couldn't have weighed more than forty pounds. Stick-thin and mal-nourished. Court Spicer's doing, the son of a bitch.

Casey was still calling her son's name. It sounded as though she was on the access lane, not far away.

"Don't make me go back there with her," the boy said. "I hate her."

"She's your mother, Kevin."

"But *he's* not my father. He's not, he's not!"

Fallon held him gently for a few seconds, to calm him, before he said, "When I set you down, stand on your good leg and lean against me. There . . . that's it. Can you walk?"

He couldn't. His injured leg buckled when he tried to put weight on it. Fallon said, "I'll have to carry you," and swung him up again, into the crook of his left arm, then reached down for the six-cell.

The flash beam, and Casey's voice calling his name now alternately with Kevin's, showed him the way to the lane. The boy clung to him, the asthma inhaler clenched tight in his hand. He was breathing more easily now, but his small body had a corded feel and was racked with small tremors.

"Kevin, why were you running away?"

"I couldn't stay there anymore. Not with *him*."

"Vernon Young? Did he do something to you?"

"No. No."

"Then what happened to make you run?"

No answer, just a shuddery inhalation.

Casey's light was visible as they neared the lane. When they came out, she was only twenty yards away. She saw them and broke into an unsteady run.

"Kevin! Oh my God, is he hurt?"

"Turned his ankle."

She tried to take the boy into her arms. Kevin went taut as a bowstring when she touched him. He said, "No!" and pressed his face against Fallon's chest.

He could smell the sweat on her. Something else, too: gin fumes. He put the light on her face. Wet, ghost-pale; the hazel eyes were as wide and seemed as dark as Kevin's had in the grove. Half drunk, he thought. And still terrified.

He pushed past her, went up the road in long, hard strides. Casey hurried after him, ran up alongside and tried to touch her son again. Kevin cringed and stiffened again. Fallon turned him away from her.

When they neared the Jeep, she said, "Put him in Vernon's car, the front seat—"

"No! Don't put me in there, *don't!*"

"Please, Rick. Then give me back the keys."

Fallon said, "No. Not yet."

"Give me the keys. Move your Jeep so we can leave."

"And go where?"

"A doctor, the ER in Indio . . ."

"He doesn't need emergency treatment. And you're not going anywhere except the ranch house."

Kevin whimpered. "I don't want to go back there, I don't want to see him again."

"You won't have to see him, honey," she said. Then, to Fallon, "He's mine, I know what's best for him—"

"The hell you do."

She said with sudden fury, "Goddamn you, let me have him!" and tried to pull Kevin out of Fallon's grasp. The boy growled at her like a whipped animal. Fallon shoved her out of the way, went around to the Jeep's passenger side, got the door opened and eased Kevin down on the seat. At first Casey clawed at him from behind, her nails once raking the side of his neck. But as soon as he shut the boy inside, she quit fighting and backed off. When he turned to shine the six-cell on her again, she was standing with her arms down at her sides, breathing in ragged little gasps. All at once, for a reason he couldn't fathom, the anger and the fear seemed to have gone out of her. Her face had a blank look, like a slate that had been wiped clean.

Fallon said, "You wanted the keys? All right, here they are." He pressed them into her sweaty hand. "Turn the car around and drive to the house. I'll follow you."

She just stood there, staring at him.

"Go on. Don't give me any more argument."

It was as if he'd pushed a button or thrown a switch to activate a mechanical device. She pivoted, slow, and walked to the BMW and closed herself inside. The engine throbbed into life. He waited until she backed up and was starting to turn before he slid into the Jeep.

The lane ran straight through the date groves for a tenth of a mile, then jogged left and widened out into a broad clearing. The ranch buildings were just beyond, packing and storage sheds first, all of them dark, the ranch house some distance beyond. The house showed lights inside and out, enough illumination for Fallon to tell that it was a rectangular, tile-roofed adobe with ornate iron balconies at the second-floor corners and outside staircases leading up to them. A four-foot-high adobe wall extended from the far corner to the edge of another date grove.

Casey bypassed a parking area in front, stopped alongside a gate in the adobe wall. Fallon pulled up behind her. Kevin stirred and made another small whimpering noise. "Do I have to go in there?"

"I won't let anything happen to you."

"I don't want to see him again."

"You won't have to. I promise."

Fallon went around to lift the boy out. Casey had the gate open; she didn't say a word, just started inside. The wall enclosed a nightlit patio garden with a swimming pool at one end—a night image of the scene in her stash of photographs. Sweet peas on trellises and some kind of white-flowered shrubs dominated the garden, their combined scents heavy in the warm night.

Two pairs of glass-paned doors, both closed, gave access to the house. Casey walked to the second, opposite the pool, and opened them and led the way down a tile-floored hall and through a doorway. She turned on the lights. Bedroom, with a single bed covered by a Mexican blanket. Kevin's room while they'd been here: some of his clothing was neatly folded on the bureau.

Fallon laid him gently on the bed, sat down to untie the laces on his right sneaker. The ankle was already starting to swell. He spread the shoe wide open, eased it and the sock off as carefully as he could. The bruise from the instep to the ankle bone was already starting to discolor.

Casey stood watching him. She hadn't said a word and her expression was still as blank as it had become on the road. Kevin wouldn't look at her. Most of the time he lay unmoving with his eyes shut.

Fallon said, "Get some ice. And a towel to wrap it in."

She went out, neither hurrying nor taking her time. Fallon sat beside the boy, smoothing the damp hair off his forehead. Warm, a little feverish. The thin lips were cracked and dry. The dark eyes looked up at him with a mixture of fright, pain, and need. Christ, what these people had done to him! Spicer, Young, Casey too in some way he didn't understand yet.

She seemed to be taking a long time getting what he'd sent her after. Fallon was about to go looking when she came in with a hand towel and the ice in a mixing bowl. He spilled some of the ice into the towel, wrapped it around the swelling ankle, then covered Kevin with the bedsheet. He smiled at the boy, smoothed his forehead again. Those frightened, needy eyes had put a lump in his throat that he couldn't seem to swallow.

He took Casey's arm and prodded her out into the hallway, shutting the door behind them. "All right. Where's Young?"

"In the front room." Dull, flat voice.

"Show me."

She led him through the house to a broad room with a black-throated stone fireplace and heavy Spanish-style furniture. Five feet into it, Fallon stopped abruptly. Casey moved around behind him, but his gaze held steady on the tile floor in front of the hearth.

An Indian throw rug was bunched up there, and sprawled on top of it was a man dressed in beige slacks and a blue shirt. The wavy brown hair on the back of the man's head was bright with blood. More blood stained the rug, the tiles, the raised hearthstone.

"I killed him," Casey said in her empty voice. "The only man I ever loved, and I killed him."

TWO

FALLON CROSSED THE ROOM, bent to feel for a pulse in Vernon Young's neck. Wasted effort. The eyes were open and sightless, the mouth twisted into a rictus. The blood on his head was still wet, but he hadn't died from the wound. Spinal shock was the probable cause. The way the head was bent, the way it rolled loosely when Fallon touched it with a fingertip, told him that the upper cervical vertebrae had been cracked in the fall against the hearthstone. He hadn't been dead more than an hour.

There was a low mahogany coffee table near the body, between the hearth and a long couch. An empty, long-stemmed martini glass stood on the table; the shattered remains of another were scattered on the floor beside Young's outflung arm. Across the room, on a wet bar inlaid with colored tiles, Fallon could see a martini pitcher, bottles that would be gin and Vermouth, an open jar of olives.

He straightened, went back to where Casey was standing. She hadn't moved. The vacant eyes stared straight ahead.

"I killed him," she said again.

"Looks more like an accident to me. What happened?"

It was several seconds before she was able to push out a reply. "We were drinking . . . arguing. Kevin heard us. He came running in and threw himself at Vernon and started hitting him. Vernon slapped him and I slapped Vernon and pushed him, hard, and he . . . his foot slid on the rug and he fell. His head . . . his head . . ." A shudder went through her. "You can't imagine the sound it made. You can't imagine. As soon as I heard it I knew he was dead."

"And Kevin saw it happen."

"Yes."

"And that's why he ran away."

"I couldn't stop him, couldn't catch him. The car, Vernon's car . . ." She shook her head, looking past Fallon at the dead man. "I killed him," she said again.

He took her arm, steered her up the steps and out of the room. She let him do it without protest; she seemed to have lost all will of her own. A dining room opened on the left, dominated by a long refectory table. He sat her down in one of the chairs at the far end, where she couldn't see into the front room, and pulled a chair over and sat next to her.

"What were you and Young arguing about?"

"I started it," she said, "it was my fault. He'd done so much for Kevin and me, we'd all been through so much. I said it was time to stop hiding the truth, I begged him to let us finally be a family."

"Family?"

"Vernon was Kevin's real father."

No surprise. Fallon had already guessed it.

"He was so angry. He said we'd been over this and over it, we could never be a family. He said what he always said—he had his reputation to think of, he couldn't leave his wife because a divorce would cost him too much. He said he had blood on his hands for me now, wasn't that enough of a commitment?"

"Spicer's blood. He killed Spicer, didn't he?"

". . . How did you know Court's dead?"

"It doesn't matter. Go on."

"I said I couldn't keep on living the way I had been, even with Kevin back safe. I said . . . I don't know, I said a lot of things. He just got more angry. He said if I kept pushing him, he would admit Kevin was his and take him away from me and make him live in his house, with his wife. He said he could prove he'd been paying me support money. He said he'd get a high-powered lawyer and sue me for custody, claim I was unstable, an unfit mother."

Fallon said, "Is all of this what Kevin overheard? Why he ran in and started hitting Young?"

"Yes. The shock . . . it was too much for him. He was yelling, 'You're not my father, you killed my father! I hate you, I hate you!' " Casey shivered again. "Now he hates me too. You heard him say so."

"He didn't mean it."

"Yes he did. He'll go on hating me for the rest of his life."

No use trying to reason with her. She was too strung out, too full of guilt and self-loathing.

"Did you tell Young when you found out you were pregnant?"

"As soon as I was sure. He wanted me to have an abortion. When I wouldn't, he . . . respected my decision. And he didn't end it between us, I don't know what I'd've done if he had. He stood by me, he did the right thing."

The right thing. Sure. Monthly support payments of $1,000, no contact with his son, and Casey as his mistress for eight more years.

"Why did you marry Spicer? To give the boy a name?"

"Yes."

"And you let him sleep with you before so he'd think Kevin was his."

"Yes. But I told him the truth about how it happened . . . a mistake with my birth control pills."

"So he never knew he wasn't Kevin's father."

"He suspected it. Every time he accused me of having an affair, he'd say, 'That kid's not mine, is he? He's somebody else's little bastard.' That's why he fought me in court, why he took Kevin and locked him up and half-starved him for four months—to punish me and my bastard son."

Fallon said, "Young gave you money to hire a private detective. Why wouldn't he let you have the two thousand to take to Vegas? Or did you lie to me about that too?"

"No. Vernon said it was a setup, that Court was behind it. I wouldn't be-lieve him. So I took the money . . . borrowed it. I knew he wouldn't go to the police. I lied to you about that."

"Yeah," Fallon said.

"I'm sorry. I just couldn't tell you about Vernon and me, Kevin being his son."

"No, because you were afraid I wouldn't help you if I knew the truth."

She made no reply. Her breathing seemed a little labored now.

He said, "Sunday night. After we talked, you called Young or he called you and you told him Spicer was in Laughlin. Told him Spicer was using Co-River Management as a mail drop."

"Yes."

"What else? The rape, the suicide attempt?"

"Just the rape. He . . . it made him furious. He said Court had gone too far. He said maybe he ought to go to Laughlin, rescue Kevin himself, have it out with Court."

Man up for once in his life. Hell, cowboy up. Charge in, playing the hero with a gun in his hand. Stupid.

Not that Rick Fallon had been a whole lot smarter.

Casey was saying, "I begged him to let you handle it, you'd done so much already, and finally he said he would. That's why I went to Laughlin with you. But he brooded about it and changed his mind."

"How did he find out where Spicer was living?"

"He called the head of the management company Monday morning. Re-altors with Vernon's reputation . . . it was easy for him to get the address."

Easy. And obvious, now. Fallon should have figured it out on his own; would have if he'd remembered thinking about Casey's real estate license and professional reciprocity when they arrived at Co-River Management.

He said, "So then Young drove or flew to Laughlin—"

"Drove."

"And walked into Spicer's house with a gun and confronted him."

"He didn't mean to kill him. But Court tried to grab the gun, and it . . . he said it just went off."

It just went off. The blanket excuse used by every damn fool who didn't know anything about guns and blew somebody away with one. Young hadn't meant to kill Spicer, and Casey hadn't meant to give him the push that caused him to break his neck on the hearthstone. A couple of senseless accidents. And in their wake there was wreckage—a traumatized little boy with two dead fathers and a lying mother, all of whom had betrayed him, and the mother with her zombie eyes and guilt over the death of her lover burned into her conscience.

"Did Kevin see that, too? The shooting?"

"No. He was locked in his room until Vernon let him out." The words came more slowly now. She sat slumped down in the chair, as if the alcohol effects were wearing off and she was very tired. "But he saw Court lying there dead. He was in shock, crying, when Vernon picked me up."

"He called you on your cell right after it happened, and you told him where you were."

"Yes. Oh God, I was so happy Kevin was safe. So happy then."

"And the three of you drove straight here."

"Yes."

"Why didn't you contact me? Why leave me dangling?"

"I wanted to call. Vernon wouldn't let me. He said Kevin was safe and you . . . . didn't matter anymore."

"Bullshit," Fallon said. "I mattered to him, all right. He was afraid I'd find out Spicer was dead and he was responsible."

"You did find out. You found us."

"Yeah. I found out a lot of things, some of them too late."

"I'm sorry," she said.

The hell you are, he thought.

She sighed, long-drawn and quavery. "We shouldn't have come here. I wanted to go home, or to Vegas for my car. Kevin wanted to go home. All those months being locked up like a prisoner, seeing Court dead . . . my God, what he's gone through."

"Why wouldn't Young let you go?"

"He said he wasn't ready to go back to San Diego yet, he needed time to regroup . . . there'd be nobody here but some men who take care of the date groves during the day and they wouldn't bother us. He was so upset, I'd never seen him like that before. He couldn't pull himself together. Couldn't stop drinking, talking about the blood on his hands, blaming me . . ."

Guilt. Fear. And whatever else unhinged men like Vernon Young.

"I started drinking in self-defense and couldn't stop and then to-night . . . tonight I killed him." She swallowed with visible effort. Fuzzily she said, "Can I have something to drink?"

"No more booze."

"Water. My throat's dry."

Fallon found his way to the kitchen, found a tumbler and filled it. Then he used his cell phone to call 911, gave the operator the ranch address and a brief explanation of what had happened here. He gave her his name, too; there was no way to avoid involving himself now.

When he came back into the dining room, Casey was bent forward across the table with her head pillowed on one arm. Passed out, he thought. He set the tumbler down, pulled her upright in the chair. Her head lolled to one side and he saw that her color wasn't good. He used his thumb to raise one of her eyelids. The eyeball was half rolled up, the pupil fixed and the white blood-veined.

A coldness slithered across his shoulder blades. He slapped her four times, hard. No response, other than faint moans.

He ran to where the bedrooms and master bath were at the rear. The bathroom door stood open. The reason she'd taken so long to fetch the ice for Kevin's ankle was that she'd been in here part of the time. In the sink were an empty plastic vial and a couple of small white tablets. He caught up the vial, read the label.

Ambien. Sleeping pills.

Shit! Why hadn't he seen this coming too?

He ran back to the dining room. Casey was sitting as he'd left her, head lolling, eyes shut. If she wasn't unconscious, she was close to it.

"No, goddamn it," he said to her, "you won't die this time either. Not *this* time either!"

THREE

H ER PULSE RATE WAS irregular, her breathing shallow but not overly labored—no trachea blockage. He felt her forehead, her cheeks; her body temperature didn't seem to have dropped. Again he slapped her face, rhythmically, back and forth, back and forth, the sound of the slaps echoing in the stillness. She moaned, rolled her head from side to side, finally began to struggle feebly. One of her eyelids lifted partway, then the other; her eyeballs had rolled up, showing mostly blood-flecked whites. She slurred the word "Stop."

He dragged the chair back, hauled her out of it, swung her into his arms. In the bathroom again, he put her down on her knees in front of the toilet, held her there with one hand and slapped her several more times to make sure she was still conscious. Then he tilted her head over the bowl, opened her mouth and shoved the first two fingers of the other hand into her mouth, as far down her throat as he could force them. She struggled, moaned, gagged. When he felt her convulse, he pulled his fingers out just in time to avoid the spew of vomit.

Partially dissolved pills, gin, and not much else. Not good; her stomach was mostly empty and that meant the drug had gotten into her bloodstream more quickly. He used toilet paper to wipe her mouth inside and out, then induced her to puke again. The third time he did it, nothing came up except a thin whitish foam.

She was half awake by then, groaning and muttering words that Fallon didn't listen to. He got her on her feet, but she couldn't stand or walk; he dragged her out into the hallway.

Kevin was standing in the door to his room, staring wide-eyed. "What're you doing? What's the matter with her?"

"She's sick, but she'll be all right. Go back to bed. Stay in there until help comes."

The boy was used to obeying orders. He retreated immediately, hobbling, and shut the door.

Casey stumbled in Fallon's grasp, babbled something incoherent. He tightened his hold, feeling the bitter anger rise again.

"It was never really about Kevin, was it?" he said to her. "Only you— your need, your pain. All about *you*."

She didn't hear the words. It wouldn't have mattered if she had.

Fallon walked her up and down the hall, dragging her until her legs began an automatic shuffling response, stopping every now and then to deliver more slaps. Time seemed to have slowed down to a crawl. Seconds were like minutes, minutes like hours.

Come on, come on, hurry up!

He was still walking her, still slapping color into her cheeks, when the county law and an ambulance finally arrived.

The ER doctors at the hospital in Indio flushed her system, put her on IV to rebalance the fluids and minerals in her body. Touch-and-go for a time, but they pulled her through. One of them told Fallon that the emergency procedures he'd learned in the army were the main reason she survived.

So his relationship with Casey Dunbar had come full circle, to end as it had begun—with the preservation of the life she'd tried to throw away. Or it would, if the Riverside County sheriff's people believed the truth as he told it, with only the self-incriminating details omitted.

It took a while, but they believed it.

And he was free again.

EPILOGUE
DEATH VALLEY

OCTOBER AGAIN, ANOTHER OCTOBER. Still the best month in the Valley.

He stood on the rim of the Ubehebe Crater, looking across at the orange tints the oxidizing ores gave to the dark volcanic ash of the eastern walls. The afternoon temperature was in the high eighties, just right for hiking and exploring. No tourists in the vicinity, no cars visible on the nearby roads. The only sound was the murmur of a light breeze.

Hard to believe, he was thinking, that almost a full year had passed since that night on the Indio date ranch. An eventful year in many ways. Casey had been held for psychiatric observation, charged with second-degree manslaughter in Vernon Young's death; pled no contest through her public defender, and been remanded to a state mental facility. So far, neither drugs nor psychotherapy had done much to help her overcome her severe depression and suicidal impulses. It would be a long time before she was deemed well enough for release, if she ever was. He felt sorry for her—in some ways more sorry, in some ways less, than he might have if the circumstances had been different.

For him it had been a good year. Very good. None of the small felonies he'd committed in Laughlin and Vegas and San Diego had come back to haunt him. He was still living on the other side of silence, still working for Unidyne, but he didn't mind it so much now because it was only temporary. Will Rodriguez was helping him look for another security job in one of the desert communities east and north of the L.A. basin; a position would open up eventually. And eventually, too, he'd have enough saved to buy a piece of California or Nevada desert property surrounded by nothing but open space and inhabited by creatures no larger or more dangerous than a javelina. All things considered, he was a lucky man. A damn lucky man.

He shifted his gaze to the fair-haired boy standing beside him. Kevin. His reward for all he'd done and tried to do last October, his redemption for the mistakes he'd made. His son now, by consent of the mother and by recent legal decree.

Casey had offered no objection to his petition for adoption. She had no family; and Vernon Young's widow wanted no part of her dead husband's bastard child, wouldn't even acknowledge his paternity. So either the boy grew up with Richard Fallon, a known quantity, the man who'd twice rescued her from the brink of death, or in a foster home among strangers. She was mentally competent enough to understand and accept the fact that he was the best option for Kevin's future. The children's court judge in San Diego had agreed.

He had Casey and the judge to thank, yes; but if you wanted to look at it another way, it was the Valley that had brought the boy to him. As if their relationship was the end product of a plan hatched deep inside this ancient rock and set in motion that day last October when he'd found Casey alive in the Butte Valley wash. As if all along the person he was meant to save, to be responsible for, was Kevin Andrew Spicer Fallon . . .

Kevin moved forward a pace, peering downward into the crater, and Fallon put out a restraining hand. "Don't get too close to the edge, Son."

"I won't. Wow, it sure is deep."

"Five hundred feet. And half a mile wide."

"What made it?"

"A volcanic explosion thousands of years ago. There's another, smaller crater half a mile south of here. Little Hebe."

"Can we go look at that?"

"Sure we can."

The boy grinned up at him. The grin was like Timmy's had been, an inner light that illuminated his features; it enhanced the superficial resemblance, but there was no sadness in the fact. Kevin was neither a replacement nor a substitute for his dead son. He was simply a boy in need of all that Fallon had been unable to give to Timmy—a new and different son, the second child he and Geena had never had.

It had taken a long time and a lot of patience to earn Kevin's trust, but he had it now. The terrified, bewildered eight-and-a-half-year-old hiding in the date groves had evolved into an inquisitive, more secure nine-year-old who seemed to be genuinely happy with his new life. It showed in his enthusiasm and his appetite; he'd begun to fill out, gain strength and endurance. He still hadn't forgiven his mother, refused to visit her, but he'd come around eventually. Fallon would make sure of it. No child should ever grow up hating anybody, least of all a parent.

Kevin had taken to the desert as well, all the marvels it had to offer—to Fallon's great relief. Kids who'd grown up in a dysfunctional urban environment either hated the stark landscapes and the solitude, or like him found comfort and refuge in them. The hot, dry climate was good for his asthma, too; the more he hiked out here, the better his breath control and the less he needed to use his inhaler.

Every chance Fallon had, he took Kevin exploring in the Mojave, the high desert country along the California–Nevada border, and twice now in the Valley. Kevin had been eager for this second trip—a camp out last night near Death Valley Junction, a tour of Scotty's Castle this morning, Ubehebe Crater and points west this afternoon. You looked at the wonder in his face and you knew that he, too, felt and responded to the Monument's powerful draw.

And maybe that, too, was part of a plan that had brought them together. Kindred souls, matched by a sentience beyond human comprehension. It seemed possible. Here, with the Valley spread out all around them, anything seemed possible.

When they turned away from the crater, Kevin asked, "Where're we going after Little Hebe, Rick?"

The use of his first name was by Fallon's request. He wondered, not for the first time, if someday Kevin might want to call him Dad. He wouldn't ask for it, but he'd be proud if it happened.

"Well, I thought maybe we'd hike up Wild Horse Canyon and camp there tonight. That's near the Panamints." Fallon pointed. "Those big mountains to the west."

"Sure, I know."

"Pretty rugged country over that way. You won't mind?"

"Heck, no. Didn't there used to be gold mines up there?"

"Gold mines and a boomtown called Panamint City. There's not much left now, but I'll show you the canyon where they were."

Halfway through the hike, Fallon paused to drink from his water bottle. When Kevin imitated him, even to the way he held the bottle, he smiled and thought fondly: desert rat in training. In the distance the Panamints loomed, gray and shadowed in their lower regions, golden where the sun struck their peaks and ridges.

He said, "You know, there's a Paiute legend about those mountains. It says little spirits called *Kai-nu-suvs* live deep inside them and only come out at night to ride bighorn sheep among the crags."

"You think it's true, Rick?"

"I wouldn't be surprised."

"Have you ever seen a mountain spirit?"

"No, but there's a first time for everything."

"Maybe we'll see one when we're there tonight."

"Maybe we will."

They walked on toward Little Hebe, not speaking now, both of them listening to the silence.

A NOTE ON THE AUTHOR

Bill Pronzini is the author of seventy novels, including three in collaboration with his wife, the novelist Marcia Muller, and is the creator of the popular Nameless Detective series. In May 2008, he received a Grand Master Award from the Mystery Writers of America. A six-time nominee for the Edgar Allan Poe Award, and two-time nominee for the International Association of Crime Writers' Hammett Prize (for *A Wasteland of Strangers* and *The Crimes of Jordan Wise*), Pronzini is also the recipient of three Shamus awards and the Lifetime Achievement Award from the Private Eye Writers of America. He lives in northern California.